Aren't We All?

A Comedy in Three Acts

by Frederick Lonsdale

A SAMUEL FRENCH ACTING EDITION

SAMUEL FRENCH

FOUNDED 1830

New York Hollywood London Toronto

SAMUELFRENCH.COM

GLOBE THEATRE
On Tuesday, April 10th, 1923,

Anthony Prinsep and Marie Löhr
present

AREN'T WE ALL?

A Comedy in Three Acts
by Frederick Lonsdale

(*Characters in the order of their appearance:*)

MORTON........................E. Vivian Reynolds
HON. WILLIE TATHAM ....Herbert Marshall
LADY FRINTON........................Ellis Jeffreys
ARTHUR WELLS ....Charles Hickman
MARTIN STEELE ....Patrick Gover
KITTY LAKE ....Cyllene Moxon
LORD GRENHAM......................Julian Royce
HON. MRS. W. TATHAM ....Marie Löhr
ROBERTS............................E. A. Walker
ANGELA LYNTON ....Elizabeth Chesney
REVEREND ERNEST LYNTON ....Eric Lewis
JOHN WILLOCKS.....................Martin Lewis

SYNOPSIS OF SCENERY

ACT ONE—Room in Willie Tatham's house in Mayfair. Evening.
ACT TWO—Room at Grenham Court. Afternoon. Two weeks have elapsed.
ACT THREE—The same as ACT TWO. The next morning.

3

The following is a copy of the play bill of the first per-
formance of "Aren't We All?" as produced at the Gaiety
Theatre, New York, May 21, 1923.

Charles Dillingham
presents

"AREN'T WE ALL?"

A Comedy in Three Acts
by Frederick Lonsdale

(*The characters in the order of their appearance:*)

MORTON.............................George Twade
HON. WILLIE TATHAM ....Leslie Howard
LADY FRINTON...................Mabel Terry-Lewis
ARTHUR WELLS.......................Denis Gurney
MARTIN STEEL.........................Jack Whiting
KITTY LAKE ....Roberta Beatty
LORD GRENHAM ....Cyril Maude
MARGOT TATHAM ....Alma Tell
ROBERTS...........................F. Gatenby Bell
HON. MRS. ERNEST LYNTON ......Marguerite St. John
REVEREND ERNEST LYNTON ....Harry Ashford
JOHN WILLCOCKS ....Geoffery Millar

SYNOPSIS OF SCENES

ACT ONE—Room in Willie Tatham's house in May-
    fair. Evening.
ACT TWO—Room in Grenham Court. Afternoon. Two
    weeks have elapsed.
ACT THREE—The same as ACT TWO. The next
    morning.

THEATRE ROYAL, HAYMARKET
20 June 1984
AREN'T WE ALL?

Revival of the play by Frederick Lonsdale

A Triumph Apollo/Birmingham Repertory Theatre Production, presented by Duncan C. Weldon with Paul Gregg and Lionel Becker, in association with Jerome Minskoff, by arrangement with Louis I. Michaels Ltd. in association with Proscenium Productions Ltd.

MORTON . . . . Robert Gladwell
HON. WILLIE TATHAM . . . . Francis Matthews
LADY FRINTON . . . . Claudette Colbert
ARTHUR WELLS . . . . Timothy Peters
MARTIN STEELE . . . . Ben Bazell
KITTY LAKE . . . . Annie Lambert
LORD GRENHAM . . . . Rex Harrison
HON. MRS. W. TATHAM . . . . Nicola Pagett
ROBERTS . . . . John Ingram
ANGELA LYNTON . . . . Madge Ryan
REV. ERNEST LYNTON . . . . Michael Gough
JOHN WILLOCKS . . . . John Price

Directed by Clifford Williams
Decor: Finlay James
Costumes: Judith Bland
Lighting: Mark Pritchard
Music: David Firman

AREN'T WE ALL?, by Frederick Lonsdale; directed by
Clifford Williams; sets by Finlay James; costumes by
Judith Bland; lighting by Natasha Katz; sound by Jan
Nebozenko; production stage manager, Warren Crane;
associate producers, Robert Michael Geisler and John
Roberdeau. Presented by Douglas Urbanski, Karl Alli-
son, Bryan Bantry, James M. Nederlander, in associa-
tion with Duncan C. Weldon with Paul Gregg, Lionel
Becker and Jerome Minskoff. Revived at the Brooks
Atkinson Theater, 256 West 47th Street, April 29th,
1985.

MORTON..............................Peter Pagan
HON. WILLIAM TATHAM.................Jeremy Brett
LADY FRINTON.....................Claudette Colbert
ARTHUR WELLS.................Steven Sutherland
MARTIN STEELE.................John Patrick Hurley
KITTY LAKE ....Leslie O'Hara
LORD GRENHAM ....Rex Harrison
HON. MRS. W. TATHAM ....Lynn Redgrave
ROBERTS ....George Ede
ANGELA LYNTON.....................Brenda Forbes
REVEREND ERNEST LYNTON ....George Rose
JOHN WILLOCKS ....Ned Schmidtke

The stage of the Globe Theatre, London
Set for Act I of "Aren't We All?"

Aren't We All?

ACT ONE

SCENE — *A room in WILLIE TATHAM's house in May-fair.*

TIME — *Evening.*

Music heard off L. *as curtain rises. MORTON enters* C. *with letters on a salver. He places the letters on the top end of desk,* L., *then goes to opening* L. *and looks off, watching the dancers and beating time to the music. He has the salver in his hand.*

Enter WILLIE TATHAM, C.

WILLIE. (*goes quickly to table, on which letters are lying, and looking through them*) Is this all?

MORTON. (*turning*) Yes, sir!

WILLIE. (*opens some of the letters*) You're sure there's no message or cable from my wife?

MORTON. Certain, sir! (*going up to door* C.)

WILLIE. Extraordinary! Extraordinary! Give me a whisky-and-soda, please!

MORTON. Certainly, sir. (*He goes to table up* R. *above fireplace and pours whisky into a glass. He then puts some soda-water in. WILLIE turns to him. The music off* L. *stops.*)

WILLIE. Not too much soda. (*MORTON puts the glass on the salver and brings it over to WILLIE.*) I'm frightfully worried, Morton!

MORTON. I'm sorry, sir.

WILLIE. (*takes glass from him*) Not a word of any sort from my wife for the last eight days! (*drinks*)

MORTON. The mails from Egypt are all wrong nowadays, sir.

9

WILLIE. But I have cabled her three times and no reply! I'm terrified she's ill again!

MORTON. Then you would have heard, sir!

WILLIE. That's true! But if I don't hear to-morrow, I'll cable the manager of the hotel.

MORTON. Yes, sir. Anything else you want, sir?

WILLIE. Nothing, thank you. (*crosses over to fireplace with his glass*)

MORTON. (*walks to door* C.; *returns*) Oh! I forgot, sir, Miss Lake rang you up!

WILLIE. Did she leave any message? (*drinks*)

MORTON. I told her you were out, sir, and that you were expected back later in the evening.

WILLIE. Ho! All right. (*Having finished his drink he puts his glass down on table below the fireplace. Exit MORTON* C.)

(*Enter LADY FRINTON,* L., *comes over to WILLIE.*)

WILLIE. (*coming a step forward*) Hullo, my dear! You look wonderful; 'pon my soul, you become younger every day.

LADY FRINTON. I'm glad of that because it takes most of the day to become it!

WILLIE. (*laughs*) Splendid!

LADY FRINTON. Willie, dear, it's sweet of you to lend me your house to give this dance to-night.

WILLIE. You're not a bit grateful.

LADY FRINTON. Why do you say that?

WILLIE. Because you have asked me to it, and you know how I loathe dancing!

LADY FRINTON. Nonsense!

WILLIE. Who's here?

LADY FRINTON. Well, the usual lot. At the last moment some of them insisted on coming in fancy dress; not serious—just anything, you know. Arthur Wells, I'm told, is coming as George Robey, and Martin Steele as Charlie Chaplin, and—

WILLIE. How frightfully original!

LADY FRINTON. My dear, you are not suggesting that two men, each born with twenty thousand a year, should be expected to have heard of Mr. Clynes or Mr. Baldwin, are you?

WILLIE. I'm sorry.

LADY FRINTON. You must be more tolerant; and lots of other people—amongst them, your father!

WILLIE. You don't mean to tell me that dear old gentleman still goes out at night? (*goes back to fire*)

LADY FRINTON. I'm very worried about your father.

WILLIE. You are?

LADY FRINTON. (*sits on settee*) Remembering the affection I had for your dear mother, and you; unless your father really gets old, and soon, I fear I shall be called upon to make the supreme sacrifice.

WILLIE. What do you mean?

LADY FRINTON. I shall have to marry him!

WILLIE. Do you know anything?

LADY FRINTON. Do I? By accident, this afternoon, I met him with a young and extremely over-dressed young person—

WILLIE. (*anxiously*) Who was she?

LADY FRINTON. I don't know. But it was quite evident it was early-closing day!

WILLIE. Did he see you?

LADY FRINTON. Oh, no; I saw to that. He called a taxi, put her into it, and to my amazement said, "British Museum!"

WILLIE. Why the British Museum?

LADY FRINTON. Don't you realize, he knows perfectly well only an air raid would drive his own class into it!

WILLIE. This is very worrying, you know.

LADY FRINTON. That's not all! His photograph, the other day, was in one of the illustrated morning papers playing with two little children; underneath it was written: "The distinguished old sportsman, Lord Grenham, whose great affection for little children regularly takes him to the park."

WILLIE. Well?

LADY FRINTON. Unfortunately for him they included the nurse in the photograph.

WILLIE. But this is perfectly dreadful. (*sits on chair down* R.)

LADY FRINTON. The worst is yet to come.

WILLIE. He's going to marry her?

LADY FRINTON. The reverse; he's having dancing lessons.

WILLIE. Good God! He's fifty-nine.

LADY FRINTON. He told Mademoiselle de Salis, the dancing mistress, he was forty-six.

WILLIE. Have you danced with him?

LADY FRINTON. He becomes acutely sciatic the moment he's asked to dance with a woman over twenty-four.

WILLIE. This must be stopped!

LADY FRINTON. It must! Unless he gives me his word of honour to become, within three months, the most popular member of the Athenæum, I marry him. Tell me, any news of Margot?

WILLIE. Not a word. I'm worried out of my life.

LADY FRINTON. Poor dear, I'm sorry; but it's all right, the posts are all wrong!

WILLIE. But I got no answer to my cable. I can't understand it. I tell you I'm worried out of my life.

LADY FRINTON. I know you are, and I'm awfully sorry for you, but you must remember, if she were ill they would have cabled you. When did you hear from her last?

WILLIE. A fortnight ago. Exactly what I expected happened; the moment she arrived, everybody begging her to sing for their cursed charities. The very thing she went away to avoid.

LADY FRINTON. What a divine voice it is, though, Willie!

WILLIE. Nevertheless, I sometimes wish she had never possessed it; singing night after night for various charities was the cause of her breakdown.

LADY FRINTON. I agree. How long has she been away? (*Music off* L.)

WILLIE. Four months; and, thank heaven, only another two months and she will be home again; and I may tell you, this house, during the last four months without her, has been perfectly damnable. I've hated it!

LADY FRINTON. I'm sure you have. (*looking at picture of MARGOT over the mantelpiece*) What a dear she is!

WILLIE. Is there such a thing as a superlative angel?

LADY FRINTON. (*looks at him*) I like you for that, Willie. (*rises and moves a step to him*) Do you know, it's wonderful the way you have settled down? You were a gay lad yourself once upon a time! Tell me, how much did your past cost you?

WILLIE. My father always told me it cost less to be generous!

LADY FRINTON. Well, he knows! (*She moves a little to* R.C.)

(*Enter ARTHUR and MARTIN,* C. *ARTHUR is dressed as George Robey and MARTIN as Charlie Chaplin.*

ARTHUR comes down R.C., *MARTIN down* L.C.
WILLIE rises and comes a step forward.)

LADY FRINTON. (*seeing ARTHUR*) Isn't he sweet!

WILLIE. Congratulations. By the way, if you are asked to a dance at nine o'clock, what do you mean by coming at 10:30?

ARTHUR. These things take a little time to put on, old friend. How are you, Lady Frinton? (*They shake hands.*) Here, Willie, I say, why are you in those clothes?

WILLIE. I'll tell you if you'll tell me why you are in those.

ARTHUR. I don't know! Some one asked me to!

LADY FRINTON. What are you supposed to be, Arthur?

ARTHUR. Isn't it obvious? Chu Chin Chow!

LADY FRINTON. Then keep humming the music, dear, or we'll never know. (*ARTHUR crosses over* L. *annoyed.*)

MARTIN. (*comes forward*) How are you, Lady Frinton? (*They shake hands.*)

LADY FRINTON. Now please don't tell me who this is! (*looking at him*) I give it up!

WILLIE. Martin Steele.

LADY FRINTON. But how perfectly wonderful. And who are you supposed to be, Martin?

MARTIN. Really, Lady Frinton, really! Charlie Chaplin, of course. (*goes down* L. *imitating Charlie Chaplin's walk*)

LADY FRINTON. But isn't that interesting, and so many people have told me he was funny.

(*The music stops. Enter MORTON,* C.)

MORTON. Miss Lake!

(Enter KITTY LAKE. Exit MORTON, c.)

LADY FRINTON. Kitty dear, how delightful. You told me you were going to the country to-day.

KITTY. I altered my mind at the last moment. You wanted me to come to-night.

LADY FRINTON. Of course I did. (*KITTY looks over at ARTHUR and MARTIN. They bow.*)

KITTY. I think you are right. (*She goes over to fireplace by WILLIE.*)

ARTHUR. (*coming forward a step*) I say, I didn't want to come in these beastly things. I only put them on to oblige.

LADY FRINTON. (*moving to him*) Quite right, Arthur, you must occasionally do something to justify your existence! (*The music starts.*)

MARTIN. I say, Kitty, I was told to-day that you are going back to the stage!

KITTY. (*shakes her head*) Never, my dear. There isn't enough money in the world to even tempt me.

WILLIE. I'm sorry to hear it.

KITTY. When you have made a reputation, keep it, don't come back and lose it.

LADY FRINTON. Wise child!

MARTIN. But you wouldn't.

KITTY. Thank you, Martin, but I haven't the courage to risk it.

LADY FRINTON. (*moving across to* L.) Come along, all of you; you must come and dance. (*She goes off* L., *followed by ARTHUR and MARTIN.*)

KITTY. Yes, do let us! (*to WILLIE*) You're going to ask me?

WILLIE. I'm hopeless!

KITTY. What nonsense! We danced splendidly together the other evening.

WILLIE. Yes, because you are so good!

KITTY. Then I must be as good to-night!

WILLIE. Then I'd love to. (*They go off* L.)

(*Enter MORTON*, C., *sees WILLIE's glass is not on the
desk, sees it is on table down* R., *goes over and,
picking it up, goes up past fireplace and puts it on
tray on table above fireplace. Enter LORD GREN-
HAM,* C. *He comes down* C. *MORTON moves to
him.*)

LORD GRENHAM. Evening, Morton!

MORTON. Good evening, my lord!

LORD GRENHAM. (*listens*) The band all right!

MORTON. Very good, I think, my lord!

LORD GRENHAM. That's all right! To us young people,
the band is all important, Morton!

MORTON. (*smiles*) Yes, my lord!

LORD GRENHAM. You dance, Morton?

MORTON. My wife doesn't care for it, my lord!

LORD GRENHAM. Quite! Quite! How is my son?

MORTON. He's very well, my lord. He's dancing at the
moment!

LORD GRENHAM. Splendid! (*walks to opening and
looks into the room*) Tell me the name of the lady dancing with my son!

MORTON. Miss Lake, my lord!

LORD GRENHAM. Miss Lake! (*comes back to* C.)
You're well, I hope, Morton?

MORTON. Thank you, my lord! And I'm glad to see
your lordship looking so well!

LORD GRENHAM. I'm all right, thanks! I was too generous that day, Morton, I lent you to my son!

MORTON. It's very kind of you to say so, my lord!

LORD GRENHAM. I miss you, Morton! However, I've no doubt you are very happy, so that's everything, isn't it?

MORTON. Mrs. Lynton well, my lord?

LORD GRENHAM. Very, thanks! My sister and her husband, the Vicar, by the way, arrive next week to spend their annual holiday with me! (*He moves away* L. *MORTON smiles and turns to suppress a laugh, then turns again.*)

MORTON. Is there anything I can get you, my lord?

LORD GRENHAM. No, thanks. (*crosses* R., *picks up paper from settee and sits there*)

(*Exit MORTON,* C. *The music stops when GRENHAM picks up paper. Enter WILLIE,* L.)

WILLIE. (*crossing over to his father*) Hullo, Father, how long have you been here?

LORD GRENHAM. Just arrived, my boy, just arrived!

WILLIE. What brings you up to town?

LORD GRENHAM. Just filling my lungs with a little of the oxygen of life in preparation for my sister and her husband — the Vicar's annual visit to me!

WILLIE. Oh! Awful! I don't know how you can bear to have them with you!

LORD GRENHAM. I have to, because nobody else *will*.

WILLIE. I wouldn't, personally! Well, how are you?

LORD GRENHAM. I'm all right, my boy, still gettin' about a bit! (*takes out cigarette and commences to smoke*)

WILLIE. (*looks at him, laughs*) You're a marvel, really

you are. I was trying to remember your exact age to-day.

LORD GRENHAM. Thirty-one or thirty-two! Never more than thirty-five! So you're giving a little dance, are you!

WILLIE. I'm not. I've merely lent my house to Mary Frinton, who is.

LORD GRENHAM. There's great excitement coming to that woman one of these days; she'll pay for something, herself! (*WILLIE laughs.*) Who's here? That pretty creature, Miss Lake, coming by any chance?

WILLIE. Yes! She's already here.

LORD GRENHAM. Already here, is she? That's good! Damned attractive woman, that, Willie.

WILLIE. *And* a nice one.

LORD GRENHAM. Experience has taught me *that's* the last thing we find out. We *know* she's attractive. You get about with her a bit, don't you?

WILLIE. I meet her occasionally, if that's what you mean? (*goes down* L.)

LORD GRENHAM. That's what I mean! I saw you lunching with her in her box at the races—(*WILLIE sits on end of desk,* L., *facing LORD GRENHAM.*)

WILLIE. So were heaps of other people!

LORD GRENHAM. You dined together the other night at the Ritz.

WILLIE. If I remember rightly there were five of us dining together.

LORD GRENHAM. Numbers mean nothing to me, Willie! Many a woman has carried on a long conversation with me without opening her mouth when there have been twenty of us dining together! Tell me, is she fond of the telephone?

WILLIE. I don't know. How should I?

LORD GRENHAM. I mean, has she started to ring you up?

WILLIE. (*pause*) No!

LORD GRENHAM. Good! If she should ring you up one day and ask if you — if you could help her to find a good architect and you're prepared to find him, Willie, take my advice, have the telephone disconnected and take a long trip to Australia!

WILLIE. I should very much like to know what you are suggesting?

LORD GRENHAM. I'm suggesting, Willie, she's a damned attractive woman, and you're a foolish fellow to see so much of her!

WILLIE. You mean, I'm in love with her?

LORD GRENHAM. I have had enough experience of life to know if you *were* in love with her, that it would be waste of time to talk to you.

WILLIE. Then what *do* you mean?

LORD GRENHAM. Just simply this! Since the world began, and up to the day that the world ends, it has been arranged for us that when an attractive man and an attractive woman have the desire to meet each other, then they meet; *then*, when they have agreed that the weather for this time of the year is most unreasonable and the last novel is most indifferent, he is left with only one thing to say to her, and that is good-bye — or tell her she is the most beautiful thing he has ever seen!

WILLIE. (*with a little laugh*) Nonsense! Nonsense!

LORD GRENHAM. A Wesleyan minister once said that to me; they tell me he travels in jam now! (*another laugh from WILLIE*) And, in addition, I'm not saying a word against the dear creature, a woman of her attraction is bound to be, shall we say, sought; so, understanding as I do, I say frankly, this is not the place to ask her.

WILLIE. Indeed! Where do you suggest I should ask her? The British Museum?

LORD GRENHAM. (*innocently*) There are many more unhealthy places than the British Museum, Willie.

WILLIE. That's why you were there this afternoon, I suppose?

LORD GRENHAM. How did you know I was there?

WILLIE. One of the mummies was so depressed at seeing a man in your position with an overdressed young shop girl, she wrote and told me.

LORD GRENHAM. Mary Frinton told you.

WILLIE. How do you know?

LORD GRENHAM. The moment you said mummy! Let me tell you something about Mary Frinton. She's started at her age the ringing up business; she's got her eye on me, Willie.

WILLIE. At all events, I *think* we can leave Miss Lake alone, don't you?

LORD GRENHAM. Just as you like, my boy.

WILLIE. Don't you sometimes regret what a bad man you have been, Father?

LORD GRENHAM. (*sadly*) Often! Often! There's only one thing I regret more.

WILLIE. What's that?

LORD GRENHAM. The opportunities I have missed that would have made me a worse one.

WILLIE. I don't mean it unkindly, but I wish I could think you had done one good thing in this world.

LORD GRENHAM. Have you ever heard of the Boy Scouts?

WILLIE. Yes.

LORD GRENHAM. I was the origin of them.

WILLIE. (*amused*) In what way?

LORD GRENHAM. Before I ever accepted any amusement any one day in my life, I made it a point of honour to walk down Bond Street and hand the glad eye to three of the ugliest women I could find, thereby filling their sad hearts with pleasure, encouragement, and even that thing which I to-day live on — hope! (*The music starts.*)

WILLIE. That's pretty good.

LORD GRENHAM. Oh! I've done a lot of unadvertised good in the world, Willie! Tell me, any news of our darling Margot?

WILLIE. Not a line! Not a syllable. I'm distracted.

LORD GRENHAM. Worrying? I'm sorry for you! She was all right in her last letter.

WILLIE. Perfectly. (*takes letter out of his pocket*) Here it is. (*He crosses over to GRENHAM and hands it to him. LORD GRENHAM reads the letter.*)

LORD GRENHAM. She seems to be enjoying herself. Who's this young man she refers to several times?

WILLIE. I don't know; some fellow she's with!

LORD GRENHAM. (*reading*) "I'm ever so much better, and enjoying myself in a way. The whole thing is spoilt for me by the number of people begging me to sing. If it goes on I shall adopt some way of avoiding them. Oh, Willie, how I ache to put my arms round you and smother your dear sweet face with kisses." (*looks at him*) That's the stuff. I have always complained there are not nearly enough of those fine creatures in the world! (*hands back letter to WILLIE*)

WILLIE. She refers to you at the end. (*shows him the place and gives him the letter again*)

LORD GRENHAM. (*reading*) "As I sit here thinking of your father, I could scream with fear that there may be something in heredity!" Bless her heart, I don't blame her. (*gives him letter and pats him affectionately on the arm*) You're a damn lucky fellow; your mother and your wife are the two nicest women I have ever known.

WILLIE. (*looks at him*) I often see why women liked you so much.

LORD GRENHAM. (*rises*) Thank you, Willie. (*crosses*

over up L.) Well, I'm goin' to have a look at the little pretties. Coming?

WILLIE. Not I. Besides, I'm going to send another cable to Margot.

LORD GRENHAM. Right you are. I like these jazz dances, Willie; it doesn't matter a damn whether you can or whether you can't! (*exits* L.)

(*WILLIE goes to desk,* L., *tears off a foreign telegraph form and sits down at the desk and commences to write out a message. When WILLIE starts to write telegram, enter KITTY LAKE,* L.)

KITTY. (*at opening,* L.) Oh! I'm sorry; you're busy.

WILLIE. (*looks up*) Not at all! (*Rises; she comes to head of desk.*) Come in! Why aren't you dancing?

KITTY. (*crossing to* C.) My dear, I suppose I'm getting old, but I'm so bored with the men you meet at dances nowadays.

WILLIE. (*smiles*) I danced with you.

KITTY. But so badly.

WILLIE. (*laughs*) That's unfortunate.

KITTY. Nonsense! You don't need to dance. Oh, I forgot to tell you, I rang you up this evening, but you weren't in.

WILLIE. So my man told me. I'm sorry.

KITTY. I was dining alone, and I thought if you were, you might like to dine with me.

WILLIE. I wish I had known. I dined at the club alone.

KITTY. What a dreadful thing to think of, two people dining alone! May I have a cigarette?

WILLIE. I beg your pardon. (*takes up cigarette-box from desk and offers her one, then lights it for her; also takes one himself and smokes, puts box back on desk*)

KITTY. (*crosses over* R., *sits on settee*) Thank you. (*leans back*) My dear, I feel so dreadfully tired! Truly, do I look terribly haggard?

WILLIE. (*coming* C.) The reverse; you look charming.

KITTY. One would expect that remark from a good dancer. Look at me and tell me the truth.

WILLIE. (*looks at her*) You look very, very pretty.

KITTY. (*laughs*) That helps me through to-morrow, doesn't it? (*They look at each other. Pause. KITTY looks around the room.*) I adore your house.

WILLIE. It is nice, isn't it?

KITTY. Charming! (*sees the picture of MARGOT over the mantelpiece*) Is that your wife's picture?

WILLIE. Yes. I had her painted in fancy dress.

KITTY. But how perfectly divine!

WILLIE. You think her pretty?

KITTY. Pretty! I think her too charming.

WILLIE. So do I. Frankly, I often wonder *why* she married me.

KITTY. (*looks at him*) Pity you said that.

WILLIE. Why?

KITTY. I don't know; it makes you so ordinary.

WILLIE. I meant it.

KITTY. (*still looking at him*) Ridiculous. You know you are *most* attractive.

WILLIE. I don't, I assure you, and very few other people do, really.

KITTY. Well, that makes you even more attractive to the *few* who do, doesn't it?

WILLIE. Well, I—

KITTY. And, being a man, you don't know how frightfully nice it is to be able to say the pleasant thing, when you are compelled so often to think the other.

WILLIE. I understand that perfectly.

KITTY. You do? (*She sighs.*) Oh dear! But I should hate not to be a woman. (*looks at writing-table*) You were writing. I disturbed you. (*rises*) I'm so sorry. (*She goes up* R. *past* R. *end of settee to behind it as if to go. The music stops.*)

WILLIE. (*going up* C.) No, no, don't go.

KITTY. (*She comes down to front of settee, WILLIE with her.*) I'm not in the way?

WILLIE. Not in the least.

KITTY. And I don't bore you?

WILLIE. Pity you said that.

KITTY. Why?

WILLIE. It makes you so ordinary.

KITTY. (*laughs*) And I am.

WILLIE. (*getting near to her*) You know you're most attractive.

KITTY. But how thrilling, particularly as I had no idea you thought I was.

WILLIE. You must be told it every day.

KITTY. But I so seldom want to hear it. But you said it rather charmingly.

WILLIE. Because it's true.

KITTY. Nevertheless, I *adore* to hear you say you *think* I am. (*She takes his hand, in which he is holding a lighted cigarette.*) May I take a light off your cigarette?

(*He holds it up for her. She removes the cigarette from her mouth, looks at him appealingly. He hesitates, bends over and kisses her. The door* C. *opens and MARGOT enters. WILLIE starts and goes down* R. *past KITTY. MARGOT appears very excited and happy, but her manner at once changes as she catches sight of them embracing. She has her furs in her hands.*)

WILLIE. (*looks at her, is unable to control himself*) Margot!

MARGOT. (*coming down* C.) Won't you introduce me? (*She puts the furs on the back of the chair at desk,* L.)

WILLIE. (*crosses to* L.C. *over past KITTY to* R. *of MARGOT*) Er—er—

MARGOT. I should like to know who it is I have to thank for so admirably filling my place during my absence.

WILLIE. Margot! (*She looks at him.*) This is Miss Lake!

MARGOT. (*crosses to her, past WILLIE*) Willie, in his delight at seeing me again, has entirely forgotten to tell you who I am. I am his wife.

KITTY. I know.

MARGOT. You know! You knew he had a wife! But how interesting!

WILLIE. Margot, you must let me explain to you.

MARGOT. But you did, most lucidly, as I entered the room.

WILLIE. I admit appearances are against me, but that kiss you saw meant nothing at all.

MARGOT. I suppose it was merely your way of explaining to Miss Lake how very much you had missed me, and how glad you would be when I came home again?

WILLIE. No, no, but—

MARGOT. I am entirely to blame.

WILLIE. You? Why?

MARGOT. (*crosses over to* L.C.) It was careless of me. I ought to have knocked at my own door before I came into my own room. I ask Miss Lake's forgiveness. (*puts her bag on the desk and commences to take off her gloves*)

KITTY. (*comes forward*) I'm sorry this has happened. I should have liked you.

MARGOT. How very flattering.

KITTY. (*moving to her*) You're entitled to say what you like, of course. As a matter of fact, I envy you. I would give anything to be in a similar position myself. But, as a woman, *you* know it had nothing to do with him. I'm going to be quite frank with you. I intended it. I like him, and I didn't know you, and quite honestly you never entered my mind.

MARGOT. (*puts her gloves on the desk*) How very interesting. And, having listened to your curious explanation, you mustn't let me detain you any longer.

KITTY. (*looks at her angrily; pauses*) You must a moment longer; it isn't quite finished! To your husband, I only appeared as attractive women do to most men — nothing else.

MARGOT. Is that so, Willie?

KITTY. That's not fair; you might have waited until I had gone to ask him that question.

MARGOT. I prefer to ask him while you are here! (*to WILLIE*) Won't you answer my question? (*He looks at them both.*) Well?

WILLIE. I — I — will tell you everything later.

MARGOT. This is your only opportunity. I mean it! Do you understand, Willie?

WILLIE. Yes.

MARGOT. Well? (*The music starts.*)

WILLIE. (*shakes his head*) I'm sorry, I can't now.

MARGOT. Very well. (*She starts to move up* C. *KITTY crosses over to* R.)

WILLIE. Margot!

MARGOT. (*looking off* L.) What's that?

WILLIE. A lot of infernal idiots dancing.

KITTY. They are not coming in here.

WILLIE. I'll stop them if they do. (*crosses over to opening,* L.)

MARGOT. What are you doing?

WILLIE. We don't want every one to know!

MARGOT. Do you mean you think it's likely I will tell them? It might occur to you, Miss Lake has much more to gain by telling them than I have. (*WILLIE comes down* L. *to front of desk and sits on the end of it.*)

WILLIE. But they will notice by your manner.

MARGOT. (*smiles*) I don't think so.

(*Enter LADY FRINTON,* L., *followed by ARTHUR, who remains up* L. *above desk.*)

LADY FRINTON. (*coming* c.) Margot, my darling! (*kisses her*) But, my dear, this is the most beautiful surprise I have ever known.

MARGOT. And I'm so glad to see you. How are you, Arthur? It is Arthur, isn't it?

ARTHUR. (*coming down a little*) Yes; in the pink, and delighted to see you again.

MARGOT. Thank you.

LADY FRINTON. (*They come down* c.) Let me look at you; quite all right again?

MARGOT. Perfectly.

LADY FRINTON. But I didn't expect to see you for another two months.

MARGOT. Neither did Willie, did you, dear? (*goes down to him, and rests on the desk beside him*)

WILLIE. No.

LADY FRINTON. (*to KITTY*) Don't you think she looks splendid?

KITTY. I, unfortunately, never met Mrs. Tatham until to-night, but she certainly looks very, very splendid!

LADY FRINTON. (*moves down to MARGOT*) Wonderful!

KITTY. (*going to ARTHUR*) I have a great desire to dance. Come along.

ARTHUR. I'd love to. (*Exeunt KITTY and ARTHUR,* L.)

LADY FRINTON. Tell me, what brought you home so soon?

MARGOT. (*takes WILLIE's arm*) Does it need any telling? But I will if you like. I left Egypt because I was terribly in love.

LADY FRINTON. Of course, how stupid of me! But you must forgive me, my dear, because nowadays most people go there because they are *not*! Do come and see them all! They'd love to see you.

MARGOT. Please! I'm so tired. I've been travelling all day.

LADY FRINTON. Of course. And I'm quite sure you don't want me here. I'll come and say good-bye before I go! (*Exit LADY FRINTON,* L.)

MARGOT. (*removes her arm from WILLIE and goes* c.) Another scene in high life avoided, Willie. (*She takes off her cloak and crosses back to chair at desk. He looks at her.*) You might thank me.

WILLIE. I do, but—

MARGOT. But how are we going to avoid it in the future? However, that's for another day! (*picks up her furs from chair and her bag from the desk, and starts to walk to door up* c.) Good night!

WILLIE. (*going a step to her*) Margot!

MARGOT. (*stops* c.) Yes.

WILLIE. I can't let you go like this; you must listen.

MARGOT. Well?

WILLIE. I tell you that kiss meant nothing to me.

MARGOT. Then I deplore your intelligence when you wish it to mean nothing to me. It's meant everything to

me. Do you understand you've crushed every single hope
of happiness out of me. I stand here cold with misery.

WILLIE. Margot, please.

MARGOT. That you could have dared ask this woman
to this house, and then dared to protect her against me.

WILLIE. I couldn't do otherwise, but I give you my
word of honour, she means nothing to me. I would give
everything I possess in the world for this not to have
happened. Won't you believe me?

MARGOT. Believe you? I came back because I love you
so much. I couldn't stay away another minute from you!
All the way over on the steamer I cried out again and
again: – quicker, quicker. Each day seemed like a hun-
dred yea s, and when I reached the house I flew up the
stairs to rush into your arms with happiness, only to
find another woman in them! And, as I stand here at
this minute, I am ashamed that I can hate anyone as
much as I do you!

WILLIE. Please, please.

MARGOT. That's all I have to say. (*goes up to door,* C.)

(*The music stops. WILLIE goes a step down* L. *Enter
    LORD GRENHAM up* L.)

LORD GRENHAM. (*coming* C.) In the name of all that's
wonderful, it's Margot! Why, what's the matter?

MARGOT. Nothing, nothing! Forgive me, Willie will
explain. (*Exit MARGOT,* C.)

LORD GRENHAM. (*crossing over to fireplace*) What
the devil has happened?

WILLIE. (*going up* C.) I must go to her. Don't you go,
do you understand, don't you go! I'll tell you everything
later. (*exit WILLIE up* C.)

(*LORD GRENHAM watches WILLIE going out. Enter
LADY FRINTON, l., comes to c. LORD GREN-
HAM goes to her.*)

LADY FRINTON. Where's Margot?

LORD GRENHAM. Have you seen her?

LADY FRINTON. Yes, of course. What's the matter?

LORD GRENHAM. Mary, there's been a row.

LADY FRINTON. A row? Who with?

LORD GRENHAM. Margot and Willie.

LADY FRINTON. You don't mean it! What about?

LORD GRENHAM. What did you usually row with your
husband about?

LADY FRINTON. A woman.

LORD GRENHAM. Well, there's no exception to the
rule, even in Margot's case.

LADY FRINTON. Are you suggesting that Willie's being
his father's son?

LORD GRENHAM. The opposite! *He's* been found out.

LADY FRINTON. Poor dear Margot!

LORD GRENHAM. Poor dear Willie!

LADY FRINTON. Do you think I can do anything?

LORD GRENHAM. You can. Go home and pray for forgiveness for asking Kitty Lake to your beastly party.

LADY FRINTON. So that's what it is?

LORD GRENHAM. I imagine so. I know it would be so
in my case.

LADY FRINTON. What brutes you men really are!

LORD GRENHAM. Not at all. It's our tender moments
that tell against us! Mary, you'd better hop it. I've got
myself out of these damn difficulties many times, but
I'm not so certain I can *lie* my son out of them. However, I am going to have a dash. I may appear to be a
very indifferent parent but, believe me, I have a great

affection for Willie, and more than that, I admire his wife.

LADY FRINTON. So you should. You'll give me lunch to-morrow, and tell me all about it, you understand? (*moves a step up* L.)

LORD GRENHAM. Right you are!

LADY FRINTON. (*going another step towards opening,* L.) Oh dear, what a place this world would be if there were no men in it.

LORD GRENHAM. If that were the case, believe me, your name would head the petition.

LADY FRINTON. Well, I must go back to my guests. (*at opening,* L.)

LORD GRENHAM. And, by the way, don't let any of your comic friends come in here — they are not wanted at the moment, believe me.

LADY FRINTON. Good night, you old fool. (*exits* L.)

(*LORD GRENHAM sits on settee* R., *the* L. *end of it. Enter WILLIE,* C., *comes down* C. *to end of settee.*)

LORD GRENHAM. Come on, tell me all about it.

WILLIE. It's awful, it's terrible!

LORD GRENHAM. I know! I know! She copped you, so to speak.

WILLIE. Yes.

LORD GRENHAM. Well, come on!

WILLIE. Meaning nothing on my honour, nothing at all, I kissed her.

LORD GRENHAM. Margot didn't see you?

WILLIE. Yes.

LORD GRENHAM. I *knew* you *would* kiss her, but I never believed you could be such a fool as to let anybody see you.

WILLIE. It was done in a second. I never meant it. Oh, I can't explain. I assure you, I don't care a damn for her.

LORD GRENHAM. You needn't explain to me, I should have done exactly the same thing. I'll stand by you, Willie, but for heaven's sake, when I've got you out of this, stand by experience. Believe me, the British Museum is much more interesting than it appears from the outside.

WILLIE. I don't know that she will come down! She won't for me, so I sent a message to say you wanted to see her. She swears she's going to leave me!

LORD GRENHAM. Never take any notice of that, first words they always say.

WILLIE. But *she* means it.

LORD GRENHAM. Nonsense! You leave it to me. I'll tell her the tale.

WILLIE. You'll do nothing of the sort. I only want you to tell her the truth.

LORD GRENHAM. My boy, there are more men separated from their wives whom they love, for that crime, than you and I could ever count. The most fatal thing in the world, believe me. Put out some of the lights, let the atmosphere be sympathetic. (*WILLIE goes down to fireplace and switches off some of the lights. LORD GRENHAM takes out a cigarette and lights it.*) Good! (*WILLIE sits down on armchair below fireplace.*) Now, quiet a moment, I must try and get myself in the frame of mind that you have done something I could never think of doing. (*The door opens—enter MARGOT,* c.) Thank you, Margot. Come over here. (*He moves to the right end of settee to make room for her beside him. She ignores this and remains standing.*)

MARGOT. (*standing by settee*) Well!

LORD GRENHAM. This is really a most regrettable and unfortunate business, my dear.

MARGOT. Have you sent for me to tell me that?

LORD GRENHAM. Certainly not. I want to help you to put it right.

MARGOT. And you think you'll be able to?

LORD GRENHAM. I'm confident.

MARGOT. Well, you're wrong. I've made up my mind.

LORD GRENHAM. Come, come, that's usually the act of a person who hasn't any, and that doesn't apply to you! Willie never meant anything by that kiss.

MARGOT. So he tells me.

LORD GRENHAM. And you don't believe him?

MARGOT. Do you?

LORD GRENHAM. Absolutely!

MARGOT. How interesting! I should have thought you the *one* man in the world who would have known better.

LORD GRENHAM. My dear, an innocent kiss, bah! What is that in a man's life?

MARGOT. Everything! should you happen to be the woman who doesn't receive it. (*moves away a step* L.C.)

LORD GRENHAM. Willie! Now, on your honour, have you ever kissed that girl before, or any other during Margot's absence?

WILLIE. (*rises*) Never, never, on my honour!

LORD GRENHAM. There you are! And I'll come out in the open. I don't know how you have done it. (*to MAR-GOT*) The whole thing may be described as an accident.

MARGOT. I'm very tired. Is there anything else?

WILLIE. Margot, my darling, please try and understand.

MARGOT. What is there to understand?

WILLIE. Don't you realize that—

MARGOT. I realize a number of ridiculous people in ridiculous clothing being entertained in my house, as an excuse for a notorious young person to be included amongst them, with the knowledge of who she is and what she is, without even the association of a delicate atmosphere. I enter the room, and it might have been some one else, and find you kissing her! That I can neither understand nor forgive. (*goes up*)

LORD GRENHAM. Well, I don't agree with you, and if you will allow me to say so, it's particularly small and un-understanding of you. (*The music starts.*)

MARGOT. (*turns*) You dare say that to me?

LORD GRENHAM. I dare!

MARGOT. Then you ought to be ashamed of yourself.

LORD GRENHAM. I'm not! And I repeat it's very unworthy of you and I am deeply disappointed in you.

WILLIE. Father, please!

LORD GRENHAM. (*rising*) My dear boy, Margot is a girl who evidently is unable to understand anything.

MARGOT. Indeed!

LORD GRENHAM. Do you deny it?

MARGOT. Absolutely!

LORD GRENHAM. Then what could you understand?

MARGOT. Many things! If it had been a garden of warmth and beauty, a wonderful moon, for instance, shining on the water and in the distance a violin playing the most divine music, and she had been an attractive woman, then I *might* have understood! (*She exits* C. *LORD GRENHAM turns to WILLIE.*)

LORD GRENHAM. It sounds attractive, but I still stand by Museums.

CURTAIN

The average time occupied in playing this Act is thirty-two minutes.

ACT TWO

SCENE — *Room at LORD GRENHAM's.*

TIME — *Afternoon. Two weeks have elapsed.*

*LORD GRENHAM enters as the curtain rises; he places
his hat and stick on a chair* R. *of the entrance up*
R.C., *where he has come in, and picks up some letters from the writing-table* R. *and goes over to the
table up* L., *opens them. Enter ROBERTS down* R.
*with "Pall Mall" and "Evening Standard." He does
not see GRENHAM, crosses over to fireplace, sees
GRENHAM and puts the papers down on the settee.*

ROBERTS. Sorry, my lord, I didn't know you had returned.

LORD GRENHAM. (*coming to back of settee*) I came
through the garden. I noticed during my absence in
London during the last three days the position of the
furniture in this room has been changed. Why?

ROBERTS. Mrs. Lynton, my lord, ordered it to be done.

LORD GRENHAM. (*nods his head with meaning*) Ah!
A considerable improvement. Tell me, has the geographi-
cal position of any other of our rooms been altered?

ROBERTS. You will find your study also considerably
improved, my lord.

LORD GRENHAM. Ah! (*There is a pause.*)

ROBERTS. (*in a manner which suggests he has something serious to say*) My lord!

LORD GRENHAM. Yes, Roberts?

ROBERTS. Polly, the parlourmaid, has given us notice
to leave at the end of the month.

LORD GRENHAM. (*sighs*) I was afraid it was going to
be the cook!

ROBERTS. If I may say so, my lord, you will find it

35

The stage of the Globe Theatre, London
Set for Act II of "Aren't We All?"

very difficult to replace Polly. An excellent servant, my lord.

LORD GRENHAM. In that case, you might, in a subtle manner, let her know that when my sister leaves here on Monday, the furniture will be replaced to the position that she and I prefer.

ROBERTS. I will, my lord.

(*GRENHAM puts his letters down on the table up* L. *ROBERTS crosses over* R. *WILLIE enters down* R. *ROBERTS stands for him to pass, then goes off down* R.)

WILLIE. Hullo, father!

LORD GRENHAM. (*looks at him*) Hullo, Willie!

WILLIE. Had a good time in town? (*He sits down on settee* L., *gives the impression of being very depressed and miserable.*)

LORD GRENHAM. (*leaning over back of settee*) Very! (*looking at him*) To the most casual observer it is evident that during my absence our domestic relations have undergone no change?

WILLIE. None! And if there had been any chance of Margot forgiving me, your sister and that Vicar she married would have entirely disposed of it!

LORD GRENHAM. (*comes to fireplace and stands with his back to it*) It was a pity their yearly visit to me should have happened at this time.

WILLIE. (*angrily*) I wish they were in hell or anywhere except here!

LORD GRENHAM. Leave *me* something to look forward to, Willie; I may be there myself in a year or two!

WILLIE. They have never stopped praying for my misdeeds ever since you left. How glad they are my mother has been spared this unhappiness! You realize, of course, they assume the worst.

LORD GRENHAM. Half the joy of life would be gone for them if they didn't.

WILLIE. Some of these Christians are odd people.

LORD GRENHAM. I am bound to say, my boy, in moments of despair, I prefer the hearty understanding of a money-lender! But Margot doesn't take them seriously.

WILLIE. Every time either of them opens their mouth, Margot looks at me and says "There," and as I told you on the telephone this morning, Margot leaves me on Monday and goes to her mother for a month! (*in anguish*) What am I to do?

LORD GRENHAM. (*smiling*) Go to the Lakes for a month.

WILLIE. What a beastly thing to suggest!

LORD GRENHAM. Possibly! But if your wife had the slightest idea you would, her mother wouldn't see her again for years!

WILLIE. You know very little about women like Margot.

LORD GRENHAM. Very, Willie, except they are identically the same as all other women.

WILLIE. You make me laugh! Why do you suppose I married her?

LORD GRENHAM. For the same reason that every *other* man marries his wife, because she is different from any other woman he has ever known.

WILLIE. Oh, it's waste of time to talk to you.

LORD GRENHAM. (*lights a cigarette*) Not at all! Your wife leaves you for four months, returns and finds you in the arms of another woman! I am full of sympathy! But, since her return a fortnight ago, despite every demonstration of regret and affection, she refuses even to allow you to hold her hand, let alone let you kiss her. Surely that's very like all other women, isn't it?

WILLIE. (*shakes his head*) Don't you understand, with her nature she can't. I have horrified her.

LORD GRENHAM. You have done more than that.

WILLIE. What do you mean?

LORD GRENHAM. You've frightened her. She's terrified you might do it again, so she's learning you, Willie. She is slowly but surely putting you in the position of never kissing any woman but her again!

WILLIE. And I never want to.

LORD GRENHAM. A noble sentiment, but a terribly cramped position to be in, believe me.

WILLIE. (*angrily*) Unless you are prepared to discuss my wife in a very different manner from this, I'll ask you to be good enough not to discuss her at all!

LORD GRENHAM. Just as you like, Willie.

WILLIE. Margot is incapable of forgiving, because she's incapable of understanding.

LORD GRENHAM. What you wish me to believe is, that Margot, given similar circumstances, provoked by admiration, her vanity sincerely appealed to, would not do what you did?

WILLIE. (*angrily*) Certainly not! How dare you make such a suggestion?

LORD GRENHAM. I'm sorry, and I congratulate you very sincerely. Supposing some one were to suggest, under similar circumstances, your wife would be as human as you were, what would you do?

WILLIE. It if were a man, knock him down!

LORD GRENHAM. (*turning to fireplace*) An effective way of encouraging reticence! (*picks up case of pearls on mantelpiece*) Charming! For Margot!

WILLIE. Yes.

LORD GRENHAM. You must have paid quite a lot of money for these.

WILLIE. Well?

LORD GRENHAM. I'm not criticizing! I was only wondering, speaking metaphorically, of course, if a shilling cane wouldn't have been more appreciated?

(*Enter ROBERTS down* R., *leaving the door open; he is carrying tea on a tray; he places it on the small tea-table in front of chair next to table* C., *then goes between the chair and the table and off down* R. *ANGELA enters* R. *when he has placed the tea on the table. She comes to LORD GRENHAM, who meets her. ROBERTS re-enters with the cake-stand and places it on the left hand of the tea-table. WILLIE goes up to table up* L. *and sits on it; he picks up a magazine and turns over the leaves.*)

ANGELA. (*to LORD GRENHAM, offers him her cheek*) So you're back again, Grenham?

LORD GRENHAM. (*kisses ANGELA*) And delighted to see you, my dear Angela.

ANGELA. (*sitting at the tea-table*) And what have you been doing in London?

LORD GRENHAM. (*smiles*) When a man reaches a certain age, there is nothing left him but to watch what other people do.

ANGELA. (*She commences to pour out LORD GRENHAM's tea, then pours out WILLIE's.*) Do I understand you have at last reached that age?

LORD GRENHAM. Not yet! (*sits on settee*) Two lumps, please.

ANGELA. When do you propose to?

LORD GRENHAM. The day I do you will find it announced on the same page as my biography in "The Times." (*gets his tea and sits again on settee*)

ANGELA. (*to WILLIE*) Like your father in other things, you take two lumps in your tea?

WILLIE. (*angrily*) Three! (*comes down and gets his tea and a cake from the stand—returns to the table and sits as before, drinking his tea and looking at the magazine*)

ANGELA. Really! (*to LORD GRENHAM*) Does your friend, Lady Frinton, know that tea is ready? (*pours out her own tea*)

LORD GRENHAM. My experience of my friend Lady Frinton is that she knows most things.

ANGELA. She'll be some time yet, I expect. She's painting her face to make herself look beautiful for you.

LORD GRENHAM. I hope so. The fear I have is, she one day may forget to paint it.

ANGELA. Horrid woman! I don't know how you can bear to have her here!

LORD GRENHAM. It's only fair, my dear sister, you should know Lady Frinton's intentions towards me are perfectly honourable. During the last ten days she has been here she has done me the honour of asking me to be her husband three times.

ANGELA. (*puts down her cup, looks at him*) You are not thinking of doing such a terrible thing, are you?

LORD GRENHAM. All my life I have found it very difficult to refuse a woman anything; except marriage! (*WILLIE laughs.*)

ANGELA. (*looks at WILLIE*) And you, young man, would be much better employed repenting of your own sins, than laughing at your father's.

WILLIE. (*angrily*) I shall laugh exactly when I like.

ANGELA. And please don't be rude to me.

LORD GRENHAM. Inability to sacrifice one's character for good manners is hardly rudeness, my dear Angela.

ANGELA. I say he was extremely rude to me!

LORD GRENHAM. (*quietly*) No, no, only an indifferently phrased, but deserved, rebuke, my dear.

ANGELA. (*stares at WILLIE*) Really!

(*Enter LADY FRINTON down* R. *She moves to tea-table.*)

LADY FRINTON. Hullo, Grenham dear! I saw you pass my window, but I had so little on I resisted the temptation of greeting you! (*Look of horror from ANGELA. To ANGELA:*) Tea ready, dear!

ANGELA. Tea has been ready for a quarter of an hour!

LADY FRINTON. Then it's undrinkable. Ring the bell, Grenham dear, and we'll have some fresh made. (*She sits at tea-table beside ANGELA. LORD GRENHAM rings bell above fireplace.*)

ANGELA. I wonder how you people keep your servants.

LADY FRINTON. By not drinking undrinkable tea, darling, thereby not apologizing to them for being a little late.

LORD GRENHAM. I agree! (*puts back his cup on the tea-tray and sits on settee again*)

(*Enter ROBERTS down* R., *comes to LADY FRINTON.*)

LADY FRINTON. Some fresh tea, please, Roberts.

ROBERTS. Yes, my lady! (*He takes teapot. Exit ROBERTS down* R.)

LADY FRINTON. There you are! Even the ordering of a little fresh tea impresses him that we are the right people!

LORD GRENHAM. Quite right! Democracy will go no distance so long as there are democrats!

LADY FRINTON. (*smiles at LORD GRENHAM; turns to ANGELA*) Now tell me, dear, all the exciting things you have done this afternoon.

ANGELA. I rested on my bed for two hours.

LADY FRINTON. But how thrilling! And I from my bedroom window was fascinated by your dear husband, the Vicar, feeding the chickens and carrying on with all the beautiful simplicity of life. And he in return, unknown to the chickens, gazed up at my window, and was equally fascinated watching me put a little black on my eyelids.

ANGELA. Lady Frinton, my husband disapproves of that habit as strongly as I do!

LADY FRINTON. Not at all! The chickens were a mere subterfuge, the accomplices of a shy man! (*Enter ROBERTS, places tea on tray.*) Thank you, Roberts. (*ANGELA has the greatest difficulty controlling herself and commences to pour out LADY FRINTON's tea. Exit ROBERTS down* R.)

ANGELA. Kindly understand I strongly resent my husband being talked of in this manner.

LADY FRINTON. Sorry, darling, we won't do it any more. (*ANGELA is about to put sugar in LADY FRINTON's cup.*) No sugar, it ruins the figure. (*ANGELA gives LADY FRINTON her tea, and LORD GRENHAM offers her the cake-stand. She takes a biscuit — and he puts down the stand again and sits as before.*) Where's Margot? Does she know tea is ready?

WILLIE. She's having it in her room.

LADY FRINTON. Are you sure? She told me she was coming down.

WILLIE. She did? I'll go and tell her! (*rises, gets to* L. *of door* R.C.)

(*VICAR enters* R.C.)

VICAR. (*as WILLIE passes him*) Ah, Willie. (*Exit WILLIE down* R. *VICAR takes a seat on settee, sitting on* R. *of LORD GRENHAM. ANGELA pours out his tea, hands it to him and then commences to knit. She had brought this on with her and placed it on her chair when she sat down.*)

LADY FRINTON. (*as VICAR passes her*) You look worried, Vicar dear!

VICAR. I am! I am! It distresses me to see those two young people separated in this manner.

LORD GRENHAM. It's entirely Margot's fault that they are. Willie has done all he can to make it up.

VICAR. The light way you treat this matter, (*ANGELA offers a biscuit to VICAR; he refuses, saying, "No, thanks."*) Grenham, sometimes suggests to me you do not remember what your son did.

LORD GRENHAM. Of course I do, my dear friend. He kissed another woman that wasn't his wife, and his wife had the good luck to catch him at it.

VICAR. The good luck?

LORD GRENHAM. Of course! How many women of your acquaintance have had the privilege of actually catching their husbands in the arms of another woman?

VICAR. (*indignant*) The men of my acquaintance are not in the habit of doing such things, Grenham.

LORD GRENHAM. Then they have a lot to learn (*pauses*) or is it you who have?

ANGELA. He *is* my brother, but he is a very, very bad man!

LORD GRENHAM. What you don't seem to grasp, Vicar, is that Margot is not angry with Willie because he kissed another woman! She's angry with herself because he should want to.

VICAR. I must be forgiven, but I do not understand.

LORD GRENHAM. Well, if some one were to tell you that the sermon you preached last Sunday was one of the dullest he had ever heard, (*LADY FRINTON laughs.*) you'd find yourself leaving him out of your prayers that night! Vanity, the most vulnerable spot in any of us.

VICAR. Indeed! Nevertheless, I still wonder, with her noble high-minded character, if she will ever be able to forgive him.

LADY FRINTON. She'll never forget, but in time she will forgive! (*finishes her tea and puts it down on the tray*)

VICAR. Ah, my dear lady, apply it to yourself. Supposing you had gone into your room and found your husband wrapped in the arms of another woman, how would it have occurred to you?

LADY FRINTON. My husband's ideas of women were rather curious. If I had caught him in that position, I should have known at once he had at last found some one who could teach him golf.

LORD GRENHAM. (*laughs*) Mary, there are moments when I adore you.

LADY FRINTON. (*blows him a kiss*) Darling! You fill me with hope.

ANGELA. You're wasting your time, Ernest. My brother looks upon his son as a hero for having broken his dear wife's heart! Even the criminal in the dock would receive my brother's sympathy.

LORD GRENHAM. Not at all, my sympathy would entirely be with the other twelve criminals in the jury box.

VICAR. (*shakes his head*) Deplorable cynicism, Grenham, deplorable!

LORD GRENHAM. Come, come, Vicar, you take this matter too seriously. What are the facts? Willie, provoked by admiration for a beautiful woman, stands to-day in the position, but for the grace of God, you, Margot, I, and heaps of other people would be in.

VICAR. Grenham, I protest! (*He hands his cup to ANGELA, who places it on the tray. VICAR rises and moves to the fireplace.*)

LORD GRENHAM. I knew you would, my dear fellow!

VICAR. I have never even looked at any other woman but my wife in my life!

LORD GRENHAM. No more would Willie if he hadn't been caught in the act.

ANGELA. Oh you bad, bad man!

LORD GRENHAM. An understanding man, my dear, who accepts the elementary facts of life! Men and women crave for appreciation more than for anything else; it's the great driving force of the world! And in our different ways we all succumb to it. Some, instead of buying a pair of socks at the hosier's for the curate, sit at home and knit them.

ANGELA. (*stops knitting*) If you are referring to me, Grenham, I have knitted socks for many curates.

LORD GRENHAM. That's all I said, darling.

ANGELA. But understand I was not in love with them.

LORD GRENHAM. No more was Willie! But, unfortunately, he doesn't knit. (*LADY FRINTON laughs. ANGELA puts down her knitting, annoyed.*)

ANGELA. You should be ashamed of yourself laughing at him!

LADY FRINTON. (*laughs*) Can't help it, my dear. (*laughs*) Grenham in this mood tickles me to death!

LORD GRENHAM. So if we could remove for a moment conventionality, which is only a more musical word than hypocrisy, and in a spirit of tolerance realize we are all capable of falling to some form of temptation, we might

begin to understand, as I say, that even Margot given
equal provocation might have done what Willie did!

VICAR. Margot is incapable of even thinking such a
thought, and to speak of a girl with her beautiful character in that way, is a mean defence of your son, for
whom I can find no excuse.

LORD GRENHAM. Miss Lake was a beautiful woman.

VICAR. Then are we all to fall at the feet of a woman
merely because she is beautiful!

LORD GRENHAM. Some man does!

(*Enter MARGOT down* R. *with her hat in her hand and
an unstamped letter.*)

MARGOT. Some man does what? (*goes to LADY
FRINTON, kisses her, goes behind ANGELA, squeezes
the hand she offers her and goes behind settee and puts
her hat on the table there*)

LORD GRENHAM. I have been endeavouring to per-
suade our Vicar, Margot dear, that to a man, a beautiful woman, and to a woman an attractive man, makes
heaven temporarily a much nearer place than he would
have us believe it is.

MARGOT. (*looks at him*) I hope he doesn't believe you.

VICAR. I don't, my dear.

MARGOT. I'm glad! (*to LORD GRENHAM*) I am
right in saying that it was I who inspired the platitude?

LORD GRENHAM. You are.

MARGOT. (*sighs*) I would be so grateful if I might be
once left out of your conversation.

VICAR. It distresses me so much, my dear, to see you
and Willie estranged in this manner.

MARGOT. If I am unable to fill Miss Lake's place in
my husband's arms with the alacrity that Miss Lake

filled mine, I must be forgiven! Has anyone a stamp?

LORD GRENHAM. (*smiles*) Happily *I* have. (*takes out a book of stamps and hands it to her*)

MARGOT. Thank you so much! (*As she is tearing off a stamp she notices ANGELA is not knitting.*) Why, Aunt Angela, this is the first time I have seen you without your knitting. (*puts the stamped letter on the table behind her and returns the book to GRENHAM*)

ANGELA. I shall never knit again in this house.

MARGOT. Why not? (*coming down to settee and sitting on the arm*)

ANGELA. It's misunderstood!

MARGOT. (*laughs*) But how funny! By whom?

ANGELA. By your father-in-law.

MARGOT. But you surely don't take any notice of what my father-in-law says, do you? (*turns to him*) Well, what did you do in London?

LORD GRENHAM. Several things!

MARGOT. Oh!

LADY FRINTON. What I want to know is, what took you up to town so suddenly the other morning?

LORD GRENHAM. (*pauses*) The honour of a lady to whom I am very devoted!

LADY FRINTON. I knew there was a woman in it!

LORD GRENHAM. Quite, but I was not the man. The man I'm referring to in this case, wrote to me about the lady, but instead of answering his letter by post I called on him personally.

LADY FRINTON. What was the lady's name?

LORD GRENHAM. (*pauses, speaks with great meaning*) If I told, not one of you would believe me.

ANGELA. Personally, I don't wish to know. (*rises and picks up her knitting and goes behind her chair towards door* R.) I am going to fill my mind and body with purer air! Ernest, I am going to walk! (*goes off up* R.C.)

LORD GRENHAM. (*smiles at the VICAR*) Which means, Ernest, *you* are going to walk.

VICAR. But I like it, Grenham—I like it! (*To LADY FRINTON, he goes off, humming a hymn: "Come, ye thankful people, come." LADY FRINTON watches him off up* R.C., *laughing. MARGOT seats herself on the chair vacated by ANGELA and helps herself to tea.*)

MARGOT. It amazes me how those two people care to take their holidays with you.

LORD GRENHAM. The house is comfortable, the food is excellent, and in their hearts they like me well enough to come and put my house in disorder for me once a year!

MARGOT. That could be avoided by your settling down and marrying again.

LORD GRENHAM. I agree. But who would have me?

LADY FRINTON. I would.

LORD GRENHAM. Mary darling, I didn't intend you to pick me up quite so quickly.

LADY FRINTON. (*rising and crossing to him*) You may not know it, Grenham, but we are being talked about.

LORD GRENHAM. Impossible, why should we be?

LADY FRINTON. (*sitting by him on settee on his right*) Because I have seen to it that we are! For months at a time I come down here and stay here, to all intents and purposes as your lady housekeeper; did you know any woman who took on that job without being full of hope?

LORD GRENHAM. Never!

LADY FRINTON. Exactly! I only told the Vicar this afternoon how dreadfully you snored!

LORD GRENHAM. What did he say?

LADY FRINTON. He became quite animated, and asked me how I knew, and I told him because my room is next to yours.

LORD GRENHAM. But it isn't.

LADY FRINTON. The Vicar would prefer that it was, so I leave the rest to him.

LORD GRENHAM. You're a very determined party, Mary dear.

LADY FRINTON. I am; I'm very fond of you, and I have made up my mind to marry you!

LORD GRENHAM. My dear! You mustn't make up your young mind in too great a hurry, think it over and come to me in five years' time, and if you still think the same way, we'll think about it.

LADY FRINTON. It's no use, Grenham, you're for it.

LORD GRENHAM. Mary dear, I am a man of very determined character.

MARGOT. Nonsense. You've already got one foot in the registrar's office.

LADY FRINTON. (*with a sigh*) Yes, but alas the other's still firmly planted in the British Museum. (*rises and crosses* R.) Nevertheless, amongst other qualities that I possess, which I commend to you, Grenham, one is, I too am a determined character. (*exit* R.)

MARGOT. And when a woman's making up her mind — well — but she's a darling, why don't you marry her?

LORD GRENHAM. It would be wrong for a young man of my elastic propensities to marry anyone yet. Besides, I couldn't bear to part with my freedom.

MARGOT. Selfish rather, isn't it?

LORD GRENHAM. I don't think so! Didn't you enjoy yours in Egypt?

MARGOT. Do you know it never occurred to me that I had it?

LORD GRENHAM. Pity.

MARGOT. Why?

LORD GRENHAM. I would have helped you to understand and forgive Willie so much quicker.

MARGOT. I hope you haven't forgotten you promised never to return to this subject?

LORD GRENHAM. I remember! So I assume you are not yet able to forgive your erring husband?

MARGOT. For the last time, I shall forgive Willie exactly when I choose.

LORD GRENHAM. Don't leave it too late.

MARGOT. What do you mean?

LORD GRENHAM. I mean, even the novelty of making love to a charming but unreciprocative wife wears off!

MARGOT. Really! Well, I don't wish to discuss it.

(*Enter WILLIE down* R., *looks at MARGOT as he goes to behind table* C.)

LORD GRENHAM. Ah, Willie, my boy. Margot, my dear, I have just remembered, I wonder if you would do something for me?

MARGOT. That's all I live for.

LORD GRENHAM. Angel! I have a young friend of mine coming by the 4.55, and as I promised to run in and see old Garnet who is ill, it's just possible I may not be back in time to greet him, so would you give him some tea and look after him for me until I return?

WILLIE. Who is he?

LORD GRENHAM. A young man you have never met, Willie, but you'll like him.

WILLIE. (*Annoyed, he moves up stage a step.*) Thoughtful of you to ask a stranger down here in these times.

LORD GRENHAM. (*rising and going up behind settee*) Very, my dear boy. It occurred to me in London our diagnosis of Margot's case is entirely wrong; we are all of us treating her for a broken heart. Whereas—I was suddenly inspired and with joy—it's nothing of the sort!

It's just a very ordinary complaint, but to effect a cure we have only to restore to her her sense of humour. (*moves to behind MARGOT*) And I rather think our young friend might considerably help. (*He takes MAR-GOT's hand and kisses it.*) Bless you! (*Exit LORD GRENHAM up* R.C., *taking his hat and stick with him. MARGOT picks up paper from* L. *end of settee, sits* C. *of settee and commences to read.*)

WILLIE. (*coming to behind settee, right end of it*) It's no use sulking with me; it's not my fault my father's a damned fool.

MARGOT. Or yours that he ever had a son!

WILLIE. That's a charming thing to say to me.

MARGOT. Wouldn't apt be more correct?

WILLIE. Does it ever occur to you that you are my wife?

MARGOT. Oh, yes! Like yourself, on occasions.

WILLIE. Margot, I have stood all that I can stand of this attitude of yours to me, and this has got to be settled now once and for all! (*She doesn't answer.*) Put that paper down!

MARGOT. (*still reading*) I'm engrossed in a case, Willie, of a woman who forgave her husband four times, and she is now doing what she should have done the first time. (*He tears the paper out of her hand, throws it away over* R.C. *She picks up the other paper from settee, and reads.*) Well?

WILLIE. How much longer do you propose to treat me in this way?

MARGOT. I have told you that is something that I have no control over.

WILLIE. (*laughs normally*) And all because I kissed a woman once!

MARGOT. Even if it was only once, you forget I saw it,

and when you can remove from my mind the picture of Miss Lake in your arms being passionately kissed by you that once, I'll take her place.

WILLIE. It's hopeless! Can't you—can't you see that I am truly repentant?

MARGOT. Is any man truly repentant at having kissed a beautiful woman?

WILLIE. Of course!

MARGOT. All men are truly repentant at having been caught kissing one, which means they will never let it happen again.

WILLIE. It will never happen again in my case.

MARGOT. You were always a pessimist, Willie dear.

WILLIE. It's no use. I can't bear it any longer. If you can't forgive me, why not have done with it, and send me away?

MARGOT. How can I? I can't trust you.

WILLIE. There you are! There you are!

MARGOT. Willie, supposing you had come into a room, and found me being kissed in the same way as I saw you kissing Miss Lake, what would your attitude be to me?

WILLIE. Such a thing is impossible!

MARGOT. I'm not as human as you are? (*He doesn't answer.*) But supposing I had, would you have spoken to me again?

WILLIE. No, I shouldn't.

MARGOT. Then why should I?

WILLIE. Because it would be quite different.

MARGOT. In what way?

WILLIE. Because you couldn't have, unless you were in love with him, and I wasn't.

MARGOT. Oh dear, I wish men knew more about women than they do! Tell me this, what would have happened if I hadn't come back that night?

WILLIE. Nothing!

MARGOT. If you mean that, you evidently know very little about yourself or Miss Lake.

WILLIE. Don't you understand? I was lonely, bored; she was an amusing companion. I never meant anything. I swear it.

MARGOT. I admit that's the silver lining; it's always the woman's fault.

WILLIE. I wouldn't go as far as that.

MARGOT. You're not expected to! But, nevertheless, it's always the woman's fault! Shall I tell you how she got you? (*WILLIE looks at her.*) You were so unlike any other man she had ever met, it was so refreshing to be appreciated by a man merely because she was a nice woman! And when she looked at my picture she was amazed at my beauty, and told you I was one of the prettiest women she had ever seen! Did she?

WILLIE. (*hesitates*) Yes.

MARGOT. Of course! (*puts her R. hand along back of settee*) I wonder why, but that never fails with any man. (*sighs*) How angry the monkeys must be when they hear that men were descended from them!

WILLIE. (*sitting by settee, takes her hand*) Margot, I beg of you! Please! Please! (*kisses the palm of her hand*)

MARGOT. That's new, Willie! (*snatches her hand away*) Did Miss Lake teach you that?

WILLIE. (*rising and moving away* R.) Oh! Oh! Damn Miss Lake! Damn everything! (*Exit WILLIE, down* R.)

(*MARGOT watches him going out. She smiles. Enter LORD GRENHAM up* R.C. *with his hat and stick in his hand. He comes to behind table* C.)

LORD GRENHAM. Where's Willie?

MARGOT. I don't know. I only know he left me in a horrid temper.

LORD GRENHAM. (*looks at her*) Ah! I'm sorry! You won't forget to look after my young friend for me?

MARGOT. I'll give him some tea and hand him over to Willie.

LORD GRENHAM. (*moves to behind settee*) As a matter of fact, Margot, I don't think Willie will like my young friend who's coming for the week-end.

MARGOT. Why not?

LORD GRENHAM. Well, I don't know! He's a charming fellow, you know, an Australian. (*She starts a little.*) By the way, now I come to think of it, I remember he told me he was out in Egypt; and when I come to think further, it must have been about the same time as you were there.

MARGOT. (*endeavours to control her agitation*) Really? (*picks up paper*)

LORD GRENHAM. He's a charming fellow, and, as I say, I think you'll like him. (*pauses*) His name, Margot, is Willocks! (*MARGOT controls her agitation, pretending to read the paper.*) By the way, you didn't by any chance when you were out in Egypt meet a lady by the name of Margaret Spalding, did you?

MARGOT. (*very agitated*) I—I—why should I?

LORD GRENHAM. I was only wondering. This young man fell very much in love with her, and, instead of returning direct to Australia, as he told her he was going to do, he is spending a few weeks in England looking for her! (*There is a pause.*) Well, I must go! (*walks up* R.C.; *at doors* R.C.) Margot! You never know with these young men, but possibly when I return I shouldn't be a bit surprised to hear he hadn't come by the 4.55. (*Exit LORD GRENHAM up* R.C., *taking his hat and stick. She ap-*

pears very excited and agitated, throws down paper.
Rings the bell violently, then goes up L. *to large table*
up L. *and gets her hat.*)

(*Enter ROBERTS down* R.)

MARGOT. (*coming* C. *to him, quickly*) Has the car
gone to meet the 4.55 yet?

ROBERTS. Just going, madam.

MARGOT. Quickly, stop him. Don't stand looking at
me, stop him. Tell him I'm coming to the station with
him! (*Exit ROBERTS down* R.)

(*MARGOT goes up to doors* R.C., *looking off. AN-*
GELA enters down R. *immediately ROBERTS is*
off; he does not shut the door after him.)

ANGELA. I wonder after dinner if you would sing to us
that —

MARGOT. (*excitedly, coming down stage*) I shall never
sing again. (*Exit MARGOT* R. *hurriedly banging door*
after her.)

(*ANGELA turns, watches her going out, appears amazed*
at her demeanour, then sees the paper WILLIE had
previously thrown on the floor, picks it up, straight-
ens it out and puts it on the large table up L. *ROB-*
ERTS enters down R. *and is going off up* R.C. *She*
stops him.)

ANGELA. Roberts, please remove that table. (*Pointing*
to the tea-table; ROBERTS puts it under the window up
R. *and exits* R. *with the cake stand.*)

(*ANGELA moves down* L., *to the table above the fire-place and picks up her writing-pad which is lying there, and moves down to the front of the fireplace. The VICAR enters down* R., *comes to* R.C.)

VICAR. What on earth has happened to our dear Margot? She's gone off in the car without even a coat.

ANGELA. (*coming forward to him*) Stupid child, she'll catch her death of cold.

VICAR. I can't help feeling your brother has been worrying her again.

ANGELA. Ernest, I am glad we are going home on Monday.

VICAR. So am I, my dear! It's a most comfortable house to stay in, and the food is excellent, excellent, but each year I come here I realize there is no place like home! Your brother knows we haven't to be back for another week!

ANGELA. I have hinted it several times, but it appears not to interest him.

VICAR. Well, it's just as well. I shall be glad to be home again.

ANGELA. I am going to write to Miss Summers; have you any message for her?

VICAR. Tell her we are coming home on Monday, and I will attend the meeting on Thursday, and in the event of our changing our minds and staying on here another week I will let her know.

ANGELA. Very well! (*Exit ANGELA down* R.)

(*VICAR goes up to large table up* L., *humming a few bars of the hymn "Come, all ye faithful people, come"; he picks up "The Times" and his voice cracks on one of the notes as WILLIE enters down* R.)

VICAR. (*coming over to WILLIE*) Do you want "The Times," Willie?

WILLIE. No! Where is Margot? Do you know?

VICAR. She went out a moment ago in a manner that can only be described as one of great unhappiness.

WILLIE. (*starts to walk out up* R.C.) Which way did she go?

VICAR. It's no use going after her; she went in the car.

WILLIE. (*goes up to the window up* R.C.) In the car? But the car's gone to the station to meet the 4.55.

VICAR. Well, she went in it.

WILLIE. I suppose my father has been upsetting her again.

VICAR. (*looks at him*) Someone has, Willie! Someone has! (*crosses past him towards door down* R., *then turns to him*) If anyone wants me I will be in the morning-room.

WILLIE. It's unlikely you will be disturbed! (*goes up behind settee* L.; *exit VICAR down* R.)

(*Enter ROBERTS down* R., *leaving door open; goes up* C. *towards WILLIE, who meets him.*)

ROBERTS. (*carrying tray with a card on it*) I am unable to find his lordship, sir, and the gentleman has just arrived.

WILLIE. (*picks up the card: looks at it*) Oh, I know! Show him in here. (*ROBERTS goes off down* R.)

(*WILLIE reads out the name on the card, "Mr. John Willocks," and throws it on the small table* C. *by settee and crosses behind the settee to the fireplace. ROBERTS enters again as WILLIE throws down the card on to the table, followed by MR. WIL-*

*LOCKS, a good-looking man about thirty and
smartly dressed.*)

ROBERTS. (*comes to* C.) Mr. Willocks, sir! (*WIL-
LOCKS goes over to WILLIE,* L., *who meets him.
ROBERTS puts the chair — which is next to the chair by
table at settee — by the desk* R. *and exits* R.)

WILLIE. (*puts out his hand*) How do you do?

WILLOCKS. How do you do? You're Mr. Tatham?

WILLIE. That's right.

WILLOCKS. Very glad to meet you.

WILLIE. Thank you.

WILLOCKS. You probably know I am staying the week-
end with you.

WILLIE. Yes! I'm glad. My father has had to go out
and see an old friend of his, but he won't be long. Do sit
down. (*WILLOCKS pulls forward chair at table* C. *and
sits on it. WILLIE sits on the settee.*)

WILLOCKS. Thank you. I was coming by train, but it
was such a perfect afternoon, and as I want to see as
much of your English country as possible, I came by car.

WILLIE. You don't live in England, then?

WILLOCKS. No, I'm an Australian.

WILLIE. Oh! I'll ring for some tea for you.

WILLOCKS. Thank you. I had it on the way down.

WILLIE. Whisky-and-soda?

WILLOCKS. No, many thanks. What a delightful place
this is!

WILLIE. It is rather. I'm glad you like it.

WILLOCKS. I do immensely! It is exceedingly kind of
your father, to whom I am more or less a stranger, to
ask me down to stay with you.

WILLIE. Not at all.

WILLOCKS. Oh, it is. I little thought when I wrote him

that letter, I should meet anyone quite as kind as he has been to me.

WILLIE. What letter was that, Mr. Willocks?

WILLOCKS. He hasn't told you?

WILLIE. No!

WILLOCKS. Then you don't know how I met your father, Mr. Tatham?

WILLIE. No.

WILLOCKS. My introduction to your father came about in a most curious way.

WILLIE. Indeed!

WILLOCKS. (*points to whisky-and-soda*) May I change my mind and have a whisky-and-soda?

WILLIE. Please, do. (*rising and going to table at back c. pours out the drink*)

WILLOCKS. Would it bore you if I told you?

WILLIE. Not at all.

WILLOCKS. (*laughs a little sadly*) It's the only thought that's in my mind. When I was abroad, I met accidentally at my hotel a lady who also was staying there alone! (*WILLIE brings down the drink and gives it to WILLOCKS. Taking it:*) Thanks.

WILLIE. That's all right. (*sits again on settee*)

WILLOCKS. When I met her it was my intention to return home that Saturday, but she attracted me, and I liked her so much, I postponed it for a week to be with her. (*lifts his glass*) Good luck!

WILLIE. Good luck! (*taking out his case*) Cigarette?

WILLOCKS. No, thanks. (*WILLIE lights a cigarette and smokes it.*) We saw a great deal of each other, and became very friendly; it was inevitable from the beginning. I soon realized I was in love with her, and although your father differs, I shall always believe she was in love with me.

WILLIE. Well?

WILLOCKS. One morning I looked for her. She was nowhere to be found. I inquired of the manager of the hotel if he knew where she was; without a word, not a message, she had left that morning for England!

WILLIE. Extraordinary! But how does my father come into it?

WILLOCKS. Because in talking one day she mentioned his name. She appeared to know him well, so as soon as I got to London I wrote to him and asked him if he could help me by telling me where I could find her.

WILLIE. And did my father know her?

WILLOCKS. Very well.

WILLIE. (*rather bored*) Well, that's all right, then.

WILLOCKS. Not quite! He has written to her and asked her for her permission to tell me where she is before giving me the address.

WILLIE. And she will give it, of course.

WILLOCKS. I believe she will, and I hope she will! (*Having finished his drink he puts down the glass on the table beside him.*)

WILLIE. Of course she will! You had no quarrel with her?

WILLOCKS. Quarrel with her? The last night I saw her, I shall never forget. It's difficult to describe to you. But if you could imagine the most perfect garden of scent and beauty! Facing us, the reflection of a perfect moon shining on the water.

WILLIE. This wasn't Egypt, by any chance?

WILLOCKS. It was.

WILLIE. Go on.

WILLOCKS. A violin fellow, and how he could play, my word, how he could play, playing in the distance marvellously! (*He stretches his arms out.*) It was the most exquisite night I shall ever know, and as I gazed at her lying in my arms, I realized everything was in sympathy with us, everything was wonderful. And as I watched her going up the steps to her hotel, I little thought it would be the last time I would ever see her! (*He pauses — WILLIE never taking his eyes off him.*) The next morning, when I found she had gone, I decided to let her go, and return home. But as the day went on, I couldn't. I realized I couldn't live without her, so I decided to come to England to find her. Immediately on my arrival I wrote to your father. I don't know why I should bore you with all this!

WILLIE. Not at all, I may be able to help you. Was she dark?

WILLOCKS. Fair.

WILLIE. Grey eyes?

WILLOCKS. Perfect blue!

WILLIE. (*after a pause*) What makes you think she was in love with you?

WILLOCKS. A woman of her type would never kiss a man if she wasn't.

WILLIE. She kissed you?

WILLOCKS. Of course! I don't care what your father says, I know she was in love with me, but I don't know why she ran away from me.

WILLIE. You needn't despair, Mr. Willocks. You will in time!

WILLOCKS. I hope so.

WILLIE. (*rises, rings bell*) In the meantime, I'm sure you would like to be shown to your room.

WILLOCKS. Thank you, I would. (*rises*)

(*Enter ROBERTS down* R.)

WILLIE. Show Mr. Willocks to his room, Roberts!

ROBERTS. Yes, sir. (*goes off, holding the door open for WILLOCKS*)

WILLOCKS. (*following ROBERTS*) I'll see you later on.

WILLIE. You will! (*WILLOCKS exits* R. *ROBERTS closes the door.*)

(*WILLIE, evidently annoyed, walks to* C. *with the intention of going out up* R.C., *but seeing MARGOT coming, he goes to the settee and picking up the paper which is lying there, sits and starts to read. MARGOT enters, up* R.C., *hat in hand. She stands and looks at WILLIE for a moment, then round the room; she is obviously suffering great anxiety.*)

MARGOT. (*coming down* C.) Hullo!

WILLIE. (*looks at her*) Hullo!

MARGOT. Haven't you been out?

WILLIE. No! I have been sitting here the whole time.

MARGOT. Shame! It's too wonderful.

WILLIE. I had nothing to go out for.

MARGOT. I hadn't either, but I went.

WILLIE. Is the car going all right again?

MARGOT. I think so. I only went a little way in it. (*There is a pause. She watches him, hoping to find out his attitude.*) Have you a cigarette, by any chance?

WILLIE. I think so. (*puts paper down, offers her one, strikes a match and lights her cigarette and returns to his reading*)

MARGOT. Thanks. Oh! By the way, where's the young man who was coming for the week-end? (*goes away past the chair* C. *and walks round behind it*)

WILLIE. The young—oh! He's not coming.

MARGOT. Not coming? (*endeavours to appear natural*) Why not?

WILLIE. I don't know! He telephoned and asked a message to be given the Governor, something about having to sail for Australia to-morrow. I really didn't take much notice of what he said, however, he's writing!

MARGOT. (*has great difficulty in controlling her relief*) What a pity! Your father will be disappointed.

WILLIE. He may not be! (*He picks up paper again. She watches him the whole time, going behind settee, throws her hat on to the large table up* L.)

MARGOT. Willie!

WILLIE. (*indifferently*) Yes?

MARGOT. Whilst I have been out, I have been thinking.

WILLIE. Interesting.

MARGOT. You're indifferent.

WILLIE. Not at all, I am most interested.

MARGOT. I was thinking of the last words your father said to me before I went away.

WILLIE. (*bitterly*) I remember he didn't want you to go.

MARGOT. I know. He said, it was a mistake when two young and attractive people were married to each other, for either of them to go too far or be too long away from home.

WILLIE. In this case he was certainly right.

MARGOT. I was thinking what a pity it was I didn't take his advice.

WILLIE. It's a little late to trouble about that now!

MARGOT. You're not being very helpful, Willie.

WILLIE. I'm sorry. I mean to be.

MARGOT. What I want to say to you, and you're making it terribly difficult, is— (*Her eye falls on the card lying on the table; she almost utters a cry.*)

WILLIE. Well? Well?

MARGOT. (*walks away*) Oh, nothing! Some other time when you are in a less indifferent frame of mind.

WILLIE. (*puts paper down*) I should like to know

what you were going to say.

MARGOT. (*appears to be thinking*) Nothing! (*goes over to the desk* R., *and seating herself—commences to write while she is speaking*) Nothing at all really! I wonder if I have time to write a note to mother before the post goes.

WILLIE. Plenty. (*MARGOT sits at table, writing note. WILLIE watches her the whole time.*)

MARGOT. What date is Monday?

WILLIE. The third! You might tell me what you were going to say.

MARGOT. I was going to say, what a pity it was, under the circumstances, I didn't do what you did whilst I was away, because if I had, it would have helped me to understand and forgive you so much quicker.

WILLIE. Was that all?

MARGOT. That was all!

(*Enter LADY FRINTON down* R., *comes to* C.)

MARGOT. Walk to the post with me in a minute?

LADY FRINTON. Love to! Mix me a cocktail, Willie dear.

WILLIE. (*rising*) I've got to go out for a moment. (*goes over to door* R.C.) You don't mind waiting until I come back?

LADY FRINTON. As long as you are not too long. I have been talking to the Vicar for the last quarter of an hour, so I need alcoholic sustenance.

WILLIE. I won't be long! (*Exit WILLIE up* R.C. *MARGOT rushes to the door to see that he has gone, comes back to LADY FRINTON, letter in hand.*)

LADY FRINTON. (*looks at her*) Margot darling, what's the matter?

MARGOT. Listen. Quickly! Quickly! Give this note unknown to anyone to a man, someone you don't know, a
stranger! He's somewhere in the house.

LADY FRINTON. What do you mean?

MARGOT. Oh, I can't explain, but he must get that
note before I see him. Don't you understand? It's someone I knew in Egypt.

LADY FRINTON. Oh, my darling, what memories you
bring back to me.

MARGOT. Please! Please!

LADY FRINTON. Where shall I find him?

MARGOT. They have put him in the end spare room,
for certain; he may be there now! Please, I'm ruined if
he doesn't get it.

LADY FRINTON. (*crosses over to door down* R.) What
terrible things we women have to put up with. I'll find
the brute now. Don't worry, darling. (*Exit LADY
FRINTON down* R.)

(*MARGOT goes over to window* L., *looking out. GREN-
HAM enters up* R.C., *puts hat and stick on chair* R.
of doors.)

LORD GRENHAM. Well, Margot, my dear, how are
you?

MARGOT. In excellent health, helped considerably by
my excellent spirits.

LORD GRENHAM. (*sits down on settee*) That's splendid!

MARGOT. (*comes to front of table* C.) You're tired. A
cigarette? (*offers him the box on table*)

LORD GRENHAM. (*taking one*) Thank you, my dear.
(*half rises to get a match*)

MARGOT. Don't get up. I'll get you a match! (*He
watches her with an amused smile. She gets a match
from the box on the table and strikes it.*)

LORD GRENHAM. You're very thoughtful, Margot dear.

MARGOT. (*holding the match for him*) One always is, to people one likes.

LORD GRENHAM. True! True! What a wonderful day!

MARGOT. Too perfect!

LORD GRENHAM. And what have you been doing this afternoon?

MARGOT. I went for a little drive in the car, and then came back and wrote a letter.

LORD GRENHAM. Splendid! By the way, did our young friend arrive?

MARGOT. (*pretends not to understand*) Our young friend? Oh! The young Australian you expected?

LORD GRENHAM. That's the fellow.

MARGOT. No, he hasn't arrived; he's not coming!

LORD GRENHAM. Not coming?

MARGOT. (*sitting on settee on GRENHAM's* R.) So Willie tells me! Willie spoke to him on the telephone. It appears he has had a cable calling him home, and he has to leave for Australia to-morrow.

LORD GRENHAM. (*smiles*) Now isn't that splendid?

MARGOT. Why? Didn't you want him to come?

LORD GRENHAM. Very much! But I much prefer that he should go back to Australia.

MARGOT. Then why ask him here?

LORD GRENHAM. (*looks at her*) You know why I asked him here?

MARGOT. (*with a look of astonishment*) I know? How should I know?

LORD GRENHAM. My dear Margot, you can afford to be generous. I never had the slightest intention of Willie knowing.

MARGOT. Of Willie knowing what? What on earth are you talking about?

LORD GRENHAM. (*smiles*) Very well. I asked Mr. Willocks here for two reasons: one, I thought his presence might restore your sense of humour as regards Willie; and two, I preferred that he should meet you on the station platform by the 4.55 instead of in a public building possibly accompanied by your husband! I knew if you met him by the 4.55 he would immediately return to London again by the 5.20.

MARGOT. May I ask you something?

LORD GRENHAM. Please.

MARGOT. Are you mad, or doesn't drink affect your legs?

LORD GRENHAM. (*laughs*) As you like! Mr. Willocks has gone to Australia, and the incident is closed.

MARGOT. You'll pardon me, it isn't. I wish to know in what way I am concerned with Mr. Williams, or whatever his name is?

LORD GRENHAM. (*smiles*) Mr. Willocks!

MARGOT. Well? Tell me.

LORD GRENHAM. As he has gone back to Australia, is it necessary?

MARGOT. Absolutely.

LORD GRENHAM. Very well. Mr. Willocks met in Egypt while you were there a widow by the name of Margaret Spalding; he fell in love with her. Realizing it, and having behaved rather, shall we say, stupidly, and not being in love with him, but with her husband, she ran away from him.

MARGOT. But you said she was a widow.

LORD GRENHAM. *I* didn't. It was *she* who said she was a widow.

MARGOT. But how extraordinary.

LORD GRENHAM. As you say, how extraordinary! It appears she acknowledged being a personal friend of mine, and loving her dearly, instead of returning to Australia, as he told her he was going to do, he came to England to try and find her. On arrival, the first thing he did was to write to me and ask me if I knew Margaret Spalding and would I help him to find her.

MARGOT. And did you know her?

LORD GRENHAM. Yes, but not by that name.

MARGOT. But how thrilling, how did you find out you knew her?

LORD GRENHAM. Only when he described to me the garden in which they spent their last evening together, and when he described the lady to me.

MARGOT. I shan't repeat it, who was she?

LORD GRENHAM. Are you serious?

MARGOT. Of course, it's most thrilling.

LORD GRENHAM. (*after a pause*) Margot Tatham! (*There is a pause.*)

MARGOT. Are you serious? (*She looks at him.*)

LORD GRENHAM. Perfectly!

MARGOT. Would you ring the bell?

LORD GRENHAM. What for?

MARGOT. I want you to tell this story to Willie.

LORD GRENHAM. (*rises and moves towards bell as if to ring, but turns to her, moving above the settee*) Margot, don't be absurd, you wouldn't be taking this attitude if this man hadn't gone back.

MARGOT. The only regret I have is this young man has gone back! Please ring the bell.

(*Enter WILLIE up* R.C., *comes to* C.)

MARGOT. Here is Willie! Will you please tell him what you were telling me.

LORD GRENHAM. Later on, my dear. So I hear, Willie,

this young friend of mine couldn't come, after all; gone back to Australia, eh? (*WILLIE doesn't answer.*) You spoke to him on the telephone, didn't you?

WILLIE. No, I didn't really.

MARGOT. But you told me you did.

WILLIE. (*looks at her*) I had a reason for saying so. He's here!

LORD GRENHAM. (*starts*) Here? (*moves a step towards settee*)

WILLIE. He'll be down in a minute.

MARGOT. You say he's here?

WILLIE. I do.

MARGOT. What was your object in telling me he had gone back to Australia when he was here the whole time? Would you be good enough to tell me what you were suggesting?

WILLIE. (*moves a step nearer to her*) This! It will be interesting to watch the reunion of you and this man in whose arms you were lying as the dawn broke in that garden of scent and beauty.

MARGOT. In whose arms I—!

WILLIE. And who saw you for the last time as you walked up the steps of your hotel. (*She looks at him.*) You don't deny it?

MARGOT. I already have to your father, but he doesn't believe me, so I shan't risk it with you. I leave it now to Mr. Wilcox, or whatever his name is. Would you be good enough to send for him? (*WILLIE does not move. There is a pause. They look at her.*) Amongst other qualities you lack, must one include deafness?

(*WILLIE goes up to doors up* R.C. *GRENHAM goes to him. Enter LADY FRINTON down* R.)

LADY FRINTON. (*comes* C.) I posted your letter, darling; in fact, I gave it to the postman himself, curious
man, never said thank you, yes or no, or anything. Just
stared at me. I hope the fool understood what posting a
letter means! (*crosses over to fireplace*) Where's my
cocktail, Willie?

WILLIE. I'll make it in a moment.

LADY FRINTON. (*looks at them*) What is the matter
with you all?

LORD GRENHAM. (*turning to her*) Nothing, my dear
Mary, nothing at all! You would do us a great service if
you would keep the Vicar and my sister away from this
room for a few moments.

MARGOT. You will do nothing of the sort. I should
like them to be here.

LADY FRINTON. What is it all about?

MARGOT. It appears there is a man in this house at
the moment who, while in Egypt, carried on with some
woman in a way, as it is told to me, that can only be
described as disgraceful!

LADY FRINTON. (*goes behind settee*) But what has it
to do with you?

MARGOT. Only that my father-in-law and my husband
accuse me of being that woman!

LADY FRINTON. (*to GRENHAM and WILLIE, ad-
vancing a step nearer to them*) You shameful, shameful
creatures! I doubt if I can ever speak to either of you
again. (*bending over the settee to right of MARGOT
and taking her arm*) Darling, take no notice of them;
they know no better. (*whispers*) Courage, he had very
little on, but what one could see of him he looked a gentleman.

(*WILLOCKS' voice heard off down* R.)

WILLOCKS. (*off*) Where is Lord Grenham?

LADY FRINTON. (*still behind settee to right of MAR-GOT*) Courage, darling, courage! (*moves to* L. *end of the settee*)

(*WILLOCKS entering down* R., *and seeing GRENHAM, goes up to him and shaking hands.*)

WILLOCKS. How are you, Lord Grenham? (*WILLIE takes him by the arm and brings him forward to MAR-GOT who has risen and moved down a pace. GREN-HAM crosses to* R. *of WILLIE as he does so.*)

WILLIE. I don't think I need introduce you. I think you have already met the lady.

WILLOCKS. (*looks at MARGOT, hesitates a second or two*) Unhappily, I have never had that pleasure.

MARGOT. How do you do, Mr. Wilcox?

WILLOCKS. (*looking her full in the face and shaking hands*) Willocks. (*WILLIE and GRENHAM gaze at each other in astonishment.*)

CURTAIN

The average time occupied in playing this Act is forty-eight minutes.

ACT THREE

SCENE — *The same as Act Two.*
TIME — *Next morning.*
ANGELA is seated C. *of settee, knitting. The VICAR*
enters down R., *comes to* R. *of chair* C.

ANGELA. (*looks at him*) Had your breakfast?

VICAR. I could eat no breakfast.

ANGELA. (*looks at him*) I'm sorry! Why was that?

VICAR. That distressing scene which I unhappily wit-
nessed last night between Margot and Willie upset me
very much. Further, it has completely disorganized my
digestive organs.

ANGELA. Still, you wouldn't have missed it, would
you, Ernest?

VICAR. I would have given a great deal to have missed
it.

ANGELA. Well, why didn't you? You only had to leave
the room.

VICAR. It was my duty to stay. I felt my presence
might have a conciliatory effect.

ANGELA. Though I trembled with indignation at the
infamous accusation Willie made against that sweet girl,
I stayed, because I enjoyed every minute of it.

VICAR. My dear! My dear!

ANGELA. And for the same reason you stayed.

VICAR. I deny that.

ANGELA. Very well.

VICAR. I have never spent a more unpleasant evening
in my life, and so long as I live I shall never forget,
in answer to a simple remark I made, the *name* your
brother called me.

ANGELA. That's the third time you have told me that.
What did my brother call you?

74

VICAR. A name I should be sorry to use in the presence of *any* woman! (*goes up to sideboard at back* C.) I wonder if there is any bisurated magnesia in the house?

ANGELA. Not in this house. They deal with your complaint much more effectively. (*pointing to brandy-and-soda*) You'll find plenty of brandy-and-soda and, unknown to any of your parishioners, I should have one if I were you.

VICAR. (*coming down to behind chair* C.) I drink a brandy-and-soda this time in the morning! What do you mean?

ANGELA. I mean your stomach trouble this morning can be accounted for by the state of alcoholic imbecility in which you came to bed last night.

VICAR. I deny that.

ANGELA. If you like! Nevertheless, you would still be trying to get into the legs of your pyjamas if I hadn't got out of bed to direct you!

VICAR. (*comes to front of armchair*) Angela, you grossly exaggerate. I admit I did probably overstep my usual allowance, as I was unhappy and upset at the name your brother called me.

ANGELA. What *did* he call you?

VICAR. (*pauses*) It wasn't damn fool!

ANGELA. (*smiles*) Darling Grenham, he's consistently called a spade by its proper name since the age of four.

VICAR. Do you mean he was right to call me by that name?

ANGELA. *I* meant the other one, darling.

VICAR. For many reasons, Angela, I shall be glad to get you home again, and if it were not that one might be of service to this dear girl, I should leave to-day.

ANGELA. Yes, Ernest! (*She looks up from her knit-*

ting.) I suppose there is no possible chance that, after all, Margot was the girl?

VICAR. Angela! (*moves behind table* C.) Do you realize what you are saying?

ANGELA. Sorry, darling, I was only asking for information. (*She smiles.*) You know more about these things than I do.

VICAR. A girl incapable of even thinking such a thought! (*comes down* R. *of sofa*)

ANGELA. Yes. (*pause*) In a way, I am sorry it *isn't* her.

VICAR. You are sorry that—? (*She looks at him.*) You're indeed a very strange person this morning!

ANGELA. I have become honest in the night.

VICAR. Explain yourself, please.

ANGELA. (*puts her knitting down*) I mean when you reach my age, knitting, without one memory, is a dull, dull business.

VICAR. (*sits on chair* C. *by settee*) But you have me, Angela.

ANGELA. (*looks at him*) I know, darling! But that doesn't make me knit any faster.

VICAR. You are not regretting, Angela, having been a good woman?

ANGELA. I refused the only opportunity I had that would have made me anything else.

VICAR. What do you mean?

ANGELA. Do you remember Mr. Tuke?

VICAR. Archdeacon Tuke?

ANGELA. Yes, but when he was Mr. Tuke, your curate?

VICAR. Yes! Well?

ANGELA. Years ago when you were out one day visiting the poor, he called and told me how much his mother would have loved me had she known me.

VICAR. Well?

ANGELA. The following week when you were again visiting the poor, he called and told me how much his sister would have loved me had she known me.

VICAR. Go on!

ANGELA. The following week, he called and told me — (*pauses — looks at him*) — how much *he* loved me.

VICAR. (*aghast*) Tuke did?

ANGELA. Tuke did.

VICAR. What did you say to him?

ANGELA. All my inclinations were to say, (*short pause*) take a seat and tell me more!

VICAR. Angela!

ANGELA. But as I lacked courage, which so often is the only thing which divides good women from bad, I opened the door for him.

VICAR. I trust you told him exactly what you thought of him?

ANGELA. I did! I said, "Good-bye, Mr. Tuke; you'll be an archdeacon some day!" (*She shakes her head.*) And you see, I was right!

VICAR. Thank God no such incident has ever happened in my life.

ANGELA. From a remark you made last night you are more fortunate than I am; yours are yet to come.

VICAR. What remark do you refer to?

ANGELA. When falling violently into bed, you turned to me and asked me, in the most aggressive manner, if it were necessary for all Sunday School teachers to be plain.

VICAR. I meant nothing, Angela.

ANGELA. Nothing, Ernest! Nevertheless, you will find me more companionable in the years to come than you have ever found me in the years that are past.

(*Enter LORD GRENHAM up* R.C., *comes over to be-*

*hind settee, takes ANGELA's hand, which she of-
fers him as he greets her, then goes to fireplace.*)

LORD GRENHAM. Morning, Angela dear. What sort of
night, Vicar?

VICAR. Not good, Grenham.

LORD GRENHAM. (*smiles*) Ha! Sorry! I have some
excellent ginger ale downstairs bottled by the firm of
Clicquot. I would advise a glass.

VICAR. Thank you, no!

ANGELA. It would do you good, Ernest.

VICAR. Thank you, no.

LORD GRENHAM. By the way, do either of you happen
to know if to-day is Mary Frinton's birthday?

ANGELA. Does she still have a birthday?

LORD GRENHAM. I imagine she must. Telegram after
telegram is arriving for her.

ANGELA. What is happening between Willie and Margot this morning, Grenham?

LORD GRENHAM. Margot is singing in her bath, and
Willie, on reflection, is not quite so sure she is all the
things he accuses her of.

ANGELA. Do you still believe she was the woman?

LORD GRENHAM. (*shakes his head*) It will remain to
my everlasting shame that I ever believed it.

(*Enter ROBERTS down* R. *He is carrying a bunch of
flowers.*)

LORD GRENHAM. I can only look for forgiveness else-
where.

VICAR. *I* cannot understand you ever believing it.

LORD GRENHAM. I cannot understand myself!

ROBERTS. (*crossing to GRENHAM*) From Lady Frinton, my lord, with her love and happiness.

LORD GRENHAM. (*looks at him perplexed, takes them from him*) Thank her ladyship very much.

ROBERTS. I will, my lord. (*exits down* R.)

ANGELA. What does that mean?

LORD GRENHAM. (*shakes his head*) No idea.

ANGELA. How extraordinary! Do you know what it means, Ernest?

VICAR. I know nothing. I am defeated by everything. I only know I shall be glad to be home again. Mentally and physically, I don't feel at all myself.

ANGELA. I insist on your having a glass of champagne, Ernest.

VICAR. No, thank you, Angela.

ANGELA. I insist!

VICAR. (*rising and moving towards door* R.) Very well —where is it—Oh, perhaps Roberts can tell me. (*goes off* R. *calling ROBERTS*) Lord Grenham says I'm to have a glass of champagne! (*They both watch him going out, turn and smile at each other. LORD GRENHAM goes up* L. *to behind settee.*)

ANGELA. If Ernest could only humbug others as he does himself, I would be a Bishop's wife to-day.

LORD GRENHAM. (*kisses her hand, laughing*) Bless you. (*puts the flowers on the table* R. *of settee and sits in chair by it*)

ANGELA. Grenham! Was Margot the woman?

LORD GRENHAM. I wish I could convince myself she wasn't with the ease I have convinced Willie. I'm terribly, terribly worried.

ANGELA. But why? If she were the woman, it is quite evident Mr. Willocks is prepared to behave like a gentleman.

LORD GRENHAM. I admit so far his behaviour has been magnificent, but I can't help feeling Mr. Willocks is an angry man with a grievance. First, against Margot for having, he sincerely believes, fooled him, and then against me for asking him here under the pretence that I liked him, and once or twice at dinner last night I could see Margot shared that feeling with me.

ANGELA. I'm sure you're wrong.

LORD GRENHAM. I'm rather afraid I'm not. Mr. Willocks unhappily doesn't understand us. I hate to say it, but he looks upon us as rather useless people; from his point of view, it would only be a proper thing to show us up and, unless I am very much mistaken, he proposes to do that through Margot.

ANGELA. Well, the most he could do would be to tell Willie.

LORD GRENHAM. And then?

ANGELA. Well, I suppose—

LORD GRENHAM. If she was the woman, you and I know she meant nothing; she proved that by running away, but will Willie believe it was merely an innocent thing? No, my dear, he wouldn't. And Margot has too much character to live with suspicion! It should never be in the power of any man to be able to make so much trouble for a woman as Willocks can!

ANGELA. What *made* you ask him here?

LORD GRENHAM. I thought it was being clever! I intended him to arrive by one train, Margot to meet him, and send him back by the next! He came by car!

WILLOCKS. (*off* R.C.) Good morning, Roberts.

LORD GRENHAM. Here he comes. You might leave me.

(*Enter WILLOCKS up* R.C. *ANGELA rises and moves to the fireplace.*)

LORD GRENHAM. Morning, my dear fellow. I hope you slept well and were comfortable.

WILLOCKS. Many thanks, I slept splendidly. (*comes over to her*) Morning, Mrs. Lynton!

ANGELA. (*smiles at him*) Good morning! Did you see my husband as you came in?

WILLOCKS. He's sitting out on the lawn having a glass of ginger ale.

ANGELA. Did he tell you it was ginger ale?

WILLOCKS. Yes.

ANGELA. (*as she goes up to door up* R.C.) Dear Ernest. (*exit up* R.C.)

WILLOCKS. (*sitting on settee*) You have a very delightful place here, Lord Grenham.

LORD GRENHAM. Stay and enjoy it as long as you like, my boy.

WILLOCKS. I'd like to very much, but I have decided to return to Australia immediately.

LORD GRENHAM. You are not leaving us at once?

WILLOCKS. If you won't think me rude, this morning.

LORD GRENHAM. Ah! I'm sorry, very sorry!

WILLOCKS. (*speaks with meaning*) In its best sense I appreciate your kindness in asking me down. I shall carry back to Australia with me only the tenderest recollections of English hospitality.

LORD GRENHAM. And we shall always think very kindly of you.

WILLOCKS. (*smiles*) I wish I could think that! Tell me, Lord Grenham, did you ever have any leanings towards diplomacy?

LORD GRENHAM. Never, my boy! A life devoted to agriculture and women!

WILLOCKS. (*laughs*) I see!

LORD GRENHAM. Why do you ask?

WILLOCKS. Because I was wondering why you asked me down.

LORD GRENHAM. For two reasons: One (*lightly*) you're a gentleman.

WILLOCKS. And the other?

LORD GRENHAM. (*more sincerely*) You're a gentleman!

WILLOCKS. (*smiles*) It must be quite refreshing to you to sometimes fail to get your own way, Lord Grenham.

LORD GRENHAM. Meaning?

WILLOCKS. Only what I said. By the way, I understand from your son, I shall have the pleasure of his companionship to London with me.

LORD GRENHAM. Willie is going to London, is he?

WILLOCKS. Yes! (*He looks at him.*) As a man should, who is married to a wonderful woman like his wife, he appreciates the monstrous accusation he made against her last night, and recognizes only time may help her to forgive him. (*He laughs.*) Incidentally, he offered me a most generous apology.

LORD GRENHAM. And you accepted it?

WILLOCKS. (*pauses*) I sympathize with it. You see, I hate being fooled even more than he will.

LORD GRENHAM. (*looks at him*) I understand perfectly, Mr. Willocks.

WILLOCKS. You needn't look at me like that. You would feel the same in my place.

LORD GRENHAM. *I* never could be in your place.

WILLOCKS. Indeed!

LORD GRENHAM. If a lady innocently philandered with me, and, realizing I was taking her seriously, ran away from me, *I* should have the good grace to leave her alone.

WILLOCKS. Let me tell you—

(*Enter WILLIE down* R.)

WILLIE. (*nervously*) Father.

LORD GRENHAM. Yes, my dear fellow!

WILLIE. (*coming to GRENHAM*) Mr. Willocks has kindly offered to drive me up to town; under the circumstances, I think I'll go.

LORD GRENHAM. (*patting him on the arm*) Hating losing you as I do, I understand.

WILLIE. I knew you would. (*sits in chair below fireplace*)

(*Enter VICAR from up* R.C. *ANGELA follows.*)

VICAR. (*walks to GRENHAM, puts out his hand*) It is my duty, Grenham, my duty, to congratulate you! (*LORD GRENHAM rises, looks at him, then takes his hand, evidently having no idea what he is talking about. Looks at the others to see if they understand. VICAR goes up to behind settee. GRENHAM sits again.*)

ANGELA. (*walks to GRENHAM, kisses him*) You know best, darling, and I can only hope you will be very happy. (*GRENHAM looks more perplexed. ANGELA joins the VICAR up* L.)

(*Enter LADY FRINTON* R. *with copy of "The Times" in her hand. She comes to GRENHAM, who rises. WILLOCKS also rises.*)

LADY FRINTON. (*puts her arms round him, kisses him*) You darling! And to have done it in such a perfectly sweet way! (*turns to the others*) I give you my word of honour I hadn't the slightest idea until I read it in "The Times" this morning.

LORD GRENHAM. Hadn't you, Mary? May I see "The Times"?

LADY FRINTON. There! (*puts her finger on a para-*

graph) You angel! (*LORD GRENHAM comes a step down stage, LADY FRINTON with him. ANGELA and VICAR come forward, listening.*)

LORD GRENHAM. (*reads*) "A marriage has been arranged and will—" (*As he is reading MARGOT enters* R.) "shortly take place between Lord Grenham of Grenham Court, and Mary Frinton, widow of the late Sir John Frinton!" (*For a moment he looks at notice, raises his eyes and looks fixedly at MARGOT, whose face is expressionless.*)

MARGOT. I congratulate you with all my heart; you have done a very wise thing.

LORD GRENHAM. Thank you, Margot.

LADY FRINTON. Why did you do it in that divine way?

LORD GRENHAM. I didn't want to take the risk of being refused, and I realized the moment it was published in the papers there was no way out of it for either of us!

LADY FRINTON. I never wanted any way out of it, darling! Oh! I'm too happy! I have already had the most charming telegrams. (*goes a step up towards ANGELA and VICAR*) Do come and let me read them to you. You can as well, Vicar; now that you're going to be my brother-in-law, you can come into my bedroom just when you like! (*VICAR looks shocked.*) Come along. (*She goes off down* R.)

ANGELA. (*to VICAR*) We had better, I suppose. (*She follows LADY FRINTON off. VICAR follows, looking very prim, smiles for a second as he passes MARGOT, then becomes serious and goes off* R.)

LORD GRENHAM. (*to WILLIE*) I notice you haven't congratulated me, Willie?

WILLIE. Frankly, I don't know why you've done it. I thought you were perfectly happy.

LORD GRENHAM. Evidently, I wasn't. (*puts "The Times" on table* C.)

WILLIE. (*rising*) There's no reason why you should have another son, is there?

LORD GRENHAM. I can't think of any, Willie.

WILLIE. (*crosses to GRENHAM and shakes hands*) Then I hope that you'll be very happy. (*walks to MARGOT, who is standing* R.C.) I should like to see you before I go.

MARGOT. That's quite certain, Willie.

WILLIE. Thanks! (*Exit WILLIE down* R.)

LORD GRENHAM. (*shaking his head*) A strange world, a very strange world! Well! Well! Well!

MARGOT. Darling!

LORD GRENHAM. Yes.

MARGOT. I rather think Mr. Willocks is anxious to discuss English life with me from an Australian point of view.

LORD GRENHAM. Ha! I see! Very well! (*Exit LORD GRENHAM up* R.C. *There is a pause. MARGOT and WILLOCKS look at each other.*)

MARGOT. (*comes forward a step to him*) Well?

WILLOCKS. Well?

MARGOT. Do smoke.

WILLOCKS. No, many thanks. Perhaps you would like to? (*She shakes her head. There is a pause.*)

MARGOT. We may not be alone long.

WILLOCKS. I realize that.

MARGOT. You don't know how to begin? (*sits on chair* C.)

WILLOCKS. (*a after pause*) You're quite right.

MARGOT. Strange! And you've been thinking of nothing else ever since you met me in this room yesterday afternoon.

WILLOCKS. You're very observant. (*sits on settee*)

MARGOT. (*shakes her head*) Merely terribly alive to the obvious! (*She smiles at him.*) But there's one thing;

you do know the end, don't you?

WILLOCKS. Do you?

MARGOT. That, if I may say so, is even more obvious!

WILLOCKS. Do you agree with it?

MARGOT. I don't complain! I realize, from your point of view, I treated you very badly.

WILLOCKS. From any point of view, can you defend it? You deliberately set out to do it! (*She shakes her head.*) Then why Margaret Spalding?

MARGOT. Because as Margot Tatham it would appear I have a reputation as a singer. Each hotel I arrived at, I found letters from different people who had heard I was coming, asking me to sing for their various charities. I hated refusing. It became so intolerable, ill and tired I left the town suddenly, leaving no address, and went to your hotel, and for peace and quietness adopted the name of Margaret Spalding. (*He laughs.*) Then why do you think I did it?

WILLOCKS. For the amusement of making some man a bigger fool than he already was.

MARGOT. You have a much greater opinion of yourself and other men than I have, Mr. Willocks.

WILLOCKS. Then, when you got to know me, why didn't you tell me?

MARGOT. There we meet on common ground. I should have. I was frightened to. Do you imagine for a moment when I first knew you I meant to compromise myself as I have done? It started as all these ridiculous things do. It was amusing to be singled out for your attentions in preference to all the other women in the hotel! It was flattering to be told all the things about oneself that one knew were not true, but always hoped were! From a depressed being, I once again became in conceit with myself.

WILLOCKS. I meant every word I said to you.

MARGOT. Of course you did, that's why I grew to like you.

WILLOCKS. Like me? You saw me falling more and more in love with you, and you encouraged me.

MARGOT. You're perfectly right.

WILLOCKS. Why did you?

MARGOT. Mr. Willocks! How few people use the power they have over others in the right way?

WILLOCKS. And then, when it amused you no longer, laughing at me, you ran away to your husband.

MARGOT. (*shakes her head*) That isn't quite correct.

WILLOCKS. Then why did you run away?

MARGOT. Will you be generous?

WILLOCKS. Well?

MARGOT. I wanted to remain. I ran away because I was frightened to stay.

WILLOCKS. You ran away because you were frightened to stay?

MARGOT. You who read the papers must realize a great many women don't.

WILLOCKS. And now?

MARGOT. Now is quite different. I'm not frightened any longer. I only wonder why I ever was.

WILLOCKS. You're frank, at all events.

MARGOT. The sincerest form of repentance! Don't you understand, it was never real, the circumstances, the atmosphere, the loneliness, *it* was all so compelling. The moment I got on the boat to come home I realized it, so much so I meant to tell my husband everything!

WILLOCKS. Then why didn't you?

MARGOT. Because, as I entered the room, I found him doing the same thing. I was so angry, I entirely forgot I had done it.

WILLOCKS. And what prevents you telling him now?

MARGOT. Too late.

WILLOCKS. Why?

MARGOT. He'd never like me again. And to stop him liking me would be the cruellest thing I could do to him.

WILLOCKS. (*inquiringly*) Or I could do to him?

MARGOT. For you to tell him would be the cruellest thing you could do to me, and that is all that should matter to you! (*He smiles.*) Why do you smile?

WILLOCKS. I don't know; it's amusing! First of all, I liked you because you liked me, and then I hated you because you didn't, and now I'm beginning to like you all over again because you like your husband.

MARGOT. I'm glad you said that.

WILLOCKS. Why?

MARGOT. It was nice! It gives me an excuse for having liked you too much! Forgive me.

WILLOCKS. (*rising*) Easier than I can myself. (*pauses*) I meant to tell everything.

MARGOT. But I did treat you very badly.

WILLOCKS. You didn't, and even if you had that's no reason; but I was angry. I thought, like so many other women, you'd used me as something merely to pass the time.

MARGOT. (*shakes her head*) Oh, no!

WILLOCKS. I know that now.

MARGOT. (*rising and coming to him*) I want you to tell me something; it's difficult. I do hope I haven't hurt you very badly.

WILLOCKS. (*takes her hand, kisses it*) It couldn't hurt any man very much to have loved a woman as nice as you; (*looks at her*) I shall always be very grateful that I did.

MARGOT. (*looks at him, smiles*) I am sure I was right to run away.

(*WILLOCKS moves to fireplace. Enter LORD GREN-HAM up* R.C., *comes down* C. *smoking a cigarette.*)

LORD GRENHAM. I hope I don't interrupt.

WILLOCKS. The opposite. I was just going to look for you to say good-bye. Oh! by the way, you might also say good-bye to your son for me, will you? Mrs. Tatham has been telling me she doesn't want him to go to London to-day. (*pause*) And I agree.

LORD GRENHAM. My dear fellow! I forgot there was another reason why I asked you down here.

WILLOCKS. Was there? What was it?

LORD GRENHAM. I knew you were a gentleman! (*WILLOCKS laughs, crosses to GRENHAM. MARGOT moves a step* L.)

WILLOCKS. Thank you, Lord Grenham! (*puts out his hand*) Good-bye!

LORD GRENHAM. Good-bye, my dear boy, good-bye!

WILLOCKS. (*goes to MARGOT*) Good-bye, Mrs. Tatham. (*shakes hands*) I am so glad to have met you — meeting you has helped me so much to forget Margaret Spalding! Good-bye! (*She looks at him — doesn't answer.*) Good-bye! (*as he crosses GRENHAM*)

LORD GRENHAM. Not good-bye, I shall see you again. (*Exit WILLOCKS down* R. *There is a pause.*) Ah, well! Nice fellow, I like him! As a matter of fact, I could forgive any woman for liking that man. Tell me, now that our young friend has departed, what do you propose to do?

MARGOT. (*comes to GRENHAM*) Forgive Willie for ever having doubted me! Oh, this is the part of it I hate so much! The lying! The deceit! Oh, it's dreadful! I want to tell him everything!

LORD GRENHAM. If you love him, for Heaven's sake I implore you not to.

MARGOT. Oh, I'm not going to! But I wish I could! But I shall one day.

LORD GRENHAM. When?

MARGOT. When I'm old and no longer attractive! When he's old enough for understanding to have taken the place of vanity!

LORD GRENHAM. I remember the day so well. When humour takes the place of anger! When tolerance takes the place of disappointment. The young call it old age. (*sighs*) Ah, well! I'm glad it's all right! Margot, I'm right in saying it was you who put the announcement of my forthcoming marriage in "The Times"?

MARGOT. Yes.

LORD GRENHAM. A severe punishment, if I may say so.

MARGOT. You gave me away, so I gave you away. You should have told me you knew him, not bring him down here as you did.

LORD GRENHAM. I should have, but still the sentence is severe.

MARGOT. I owed it to Mary. She saved me, and the only way I could repay her was to give you to her, who for some reason she adores.

LORD GRENHAM. (*sighs; crosses to fireplace, and throws away his cigarette*) And I had planned so many interesting things to do in the next five years.

MARGOT. But you like her?

LORD GRENHAM. Enormously, but I don't want to marry her. I hate the idea of marrying anyone. I'm so used to freedom! I love it so! And married to Mary, there's going to be no more freedom! But I forgive you. But if ever you tell her that it was you who put that notice in the paper and not me, then I'll never forgive you.

(*Enter LADY FRINTON down* R. *She comes to chair* C.)

LADY FRINTON. Grenham dear, the "Daily Mirror" have just rung up to ask if we would allow their photographers to take our photographs. I said with pleasure. You don't mind, do you, darling?

LORD GRENHAM. If it will please you, I know of nothing that could give me more pleasure.

LADY FRINTON. (*to MARGOT*) Isn't he too wonderful?

MARGOT. He's a dear. (*kisses her*) I hope, and I know you will be very happy. (*Exit MARGOT up* R.C.)

LADY FRINTON. A sweet, sweet creature.

LORD GRENHAM. And a great friend of yours.

LADY FRINTON. (*cross over to GRENHAM, presses his shoulders*) I know! Grenham, you don't know how happy you have made me.

LORD GRENHAM. You flatter me, Mary dear. (*LADY FRINTON sits on settee, GRENHAM beside her, on her* L.)

LADY FRINTON. And I was beginning to give up all hope. I was beginning to think I should never get you! What made you do it so suddenly?

LORD GRENHAM. Not suddenly, my dear; after much considered thought. When a man reaches my age, he needs companionship. Living alone, not knowing what to do, becomes unbearable. I couldn't stand it any longer. And in the whole world there was only one person whose companionship I would care to share, so I advertised the fact in "The Times," and believing you felt the same way as I did, I took the liberty of including your name with mine!

LADY FRINTON. I know I shall cry.

LORD GRENHAM. It would considerably add to my happiness if you didn't, Mary dear.

LADY FRINTON. (*moves closer to him*) I won't, then. Tell me, when do you propose we should be married, Grenham?

LORD GRENHAM. That's for you to decide.

LADY FRINTON. Is a month's time too soon?

LORD GRENHAM. Will that give you sufficient time to arrange everything?

LADY FRINTON. More than enough.

LORD GRENHAM. Very well! And while you're fixing up everything, so as not to be in your way, I'll just run over to Paris for that time.

LADY FRINTON. Do!

LORD GRENHAM. (*appears surprised*) You don't mind?

LADY FRINTON. I'd like you to. And I hope, when we are married, you'll often do it.

LORD GRENHAM. Go without you, you mean!

LADY FRINTON. Of course! Whenever you want to.

LORD GRENHAM. You're being very generous, Mary dear.

LADY FRINTON. No, my dear, I'm only being very clever. Gradually it will be the cause of your staying at home, or better still, wanting to take me with you.

LORD GRENHAM. (*laughs*) I believe you're right! Mary, there is one thing about you I have always adored.

LADY FRINTON. What?

LORD GRENHAM. You make me laugh. (*LADY FRINTON laughs.*) Surely two married people can't ask for much more, can they?

LADY FRINTON. They shouldn't.

(*GRENHAM is just bending over her as ROBERTS enters down* R. *They move apart.*)

ROBERTS. Mr. Willocks is just leaving, my lord.

LORD GRENHAM. All right. I'll be there in a moment.

(*Exit ROBERTS down* R. *LADY FRINTON and GRENHAM rise, he takes her arm and they move to* R.C.) Come along, we'll go and say good-bye to him together. My age is forty-eight. How old are you, Mary dear? (*They both stop, and she whispers audibly to him* "Twenty-two," *and, laughing, they both go off down* R.)

(*Enter MARGOT up* R.C.; *stands there waving off. The car is leaving in the distance. Enter WILLIE down* R.)

WILLIE. (*watches MARGOT, who is standing at window, unaware WILLIE is in the room*) Margot!

MARGOT. (*starts*) What a fright you gave me!

WILLIE. What were you looking at?

MARGOT. I was watching Mr. Willocks going off in his car.

WILLIE. But I was going with him.

MARGOT. Apparently he's forgotten that!

WILLIE. It doesn't matter. I'll go by train.

MARGOT. (*indifferently, coming to chair* C.) I'm going by the 4.30.

WILLIE. (*comes forward to* R.C.) To London?

MARGOT. To London!

WILLIE. We might travel together?

MARGOT. If we are going by the same train, it would be ridiculous if we didn't! There is no reason to let every one know your opinion of me.

WILLIE. I have no opinion of you other than I have always had. I detest myself for ever having had any other!

MARGOT. You mean, you are sorry for all the horrid things you said to me last night?

WILLIE. As long as I live I shall never cease to regret the things I said to you. The only excuse I can find for myself is that I adore you. I was jealous of you to utter madness. But I can find no reason why you should ever forgive me!

MARGOT. And you're convinced I was not that woman?

WILLIE. I'm sure you were!

MARGOT. You're sure — (*angrily*) How dare you!

WILLIE. I should have never mentioned it if you hadn't!

MARGOT. Really! (*comes to front of table,* C.) How interesting — how terribly interesting! (*satirically*) It's sweet of you to be so nice about it.

WILLIE. Not at all; experience has taught me understanding.

MARGOT. Really! Really!

WILLIE. And something else.

MARGOT. Being?

WILLIE. If I had been out in Egypt and met Miss Lake, I should have returned to you — but I don't think I should have run away.

MARGOT. Meaning?

WILLIE. (*comes closer to her*) He was as attractive as Miss Lake, and you did?

MARGOT. Yes!

WILLIE. (*takes her hand*) And you could have stayed and I should never have known! And it was because of me you didn't!

MARGOT. Yes!

WILLIE. All people are as human as you are, but few as good!

MARGOT. Are you really being as nice to me as you appear, Willie?

WILLIE. I can never be nice enough to you. (*He takes her in his arms, kisses her and breaks away.*) What were those words my father said to you before you went away?

MARGOT. When two young and attractive people are

married to each other, it's a mistake for either of them to go too far, or be too long away from home!

WILLIE. Only the unattractive ones would refuse to agree with him! Anyway, I'll take precious good care you never go away again.

MARGOT. So will I, Willie dear!

WILLIE. We'll never get a carriage to ourselves — let's go by car, shall we?

MARGOT. Oh yes, let us!

WILLIE. I'll go and order it! (*kisses her*) Darling! (*He goes up to door,* R.C. *She goes up a step to him. LORD GRENHAM enters down* R.)

MARGOT. Willie!

WILLIE. Yes?

MARGOT. I'm so glad you know!

WILLIE. Don't I know you are! (*He blows her a kiss. Exit WILLIE up* R.C. *She stands watching him go off. GRENHAM goes over to table* C. *as if to pick up "The Times" which he had previously put down there.*)

LORD GRENHAM. Willocks has gone. Willie has gone mad, and I'm going to be married! All very strange.

MARGOT. (*coming down to him*) Willie and I are just going to London.

LORD GRENHAM. That's good, very good; I'm delighted.

MARGOT. I know you are! I may not see you again, so I'll say good-bye. (*kisses him*) You ought to be very happy.

LORD GRENHAM. Why particularly, Margot?

MARGOT. Because I'm terribly fond of you. I adore your future wife, and I love your son! (*goes up to exit* R.C., *GRENHAM following her*) Good-bye! (*Exit MARGOT up* R.C.)

LORD GRENHAM. (*coming down* C.) It's all very

strange. Very strange! (*The VICAR enters down* R. *looking very upset; he pauses at the door.*) Come in, old friend! How are you feeling?

VICAR. (*comes to* R.C.) Very much the same. I laid on my bed, but I was unable to sleep.

LORD GRENHAM. Bad luck!

VICAR. Grenham, my mind is greatly disturbed. I must speak to you.

LORD GRENHAM. But do, my dear fellow. (*He gets the chair from table at settee and places it* C. *VICAR sits there and GRENHAM moves to his* R.) Come and sit down.

VICAR. I feel I cannot eat another mouthful of bread in your house, bearing the resentment I do against you, without telling you.

LORD GRENHAM. Against me, but why?

VICAR. Have you forgotten the name you called me last night?

LORD GRENHAM. Name? I don't remember calling you any name. What was it?

VICAR. If you have forgotten, I prefer not to remind you.

LORD GRENHAM. But I insist! You hear, I insist! What was it?

VICAR. (*looks round the room to see if anyone is about — whispers*) In answer to a simple remark I made last night, Grenham, you called me a bloody old fool! (*puts his head in his hands as if crying*)

LORD GRENHAM. (*puts his arm round his shoulder*) But aren't we all, old friend?

CURTAIN

The average time occupied in playing this Act is thirty-two minutes.

PROPERTY PLOT

ACT ONE

1 large Turkey carpet square; 1 long red and black rug to fireplace; 2 small pattern rugs; 1 blue painted Aubosson square; fireplace and ormolu kerb; 1 standard set of brasses; 1 large oil-painting over fireplace, R. On fireplace—2 large brass vases and 1 French marble clock. On O.P., back flat—1 large oil-painting of Spanish lady. On P.S., back flat—1 small oil-painting of a lady playing Margot; 2 small and 1 medium commodes (on them—3 Dresden ornaments on each, and 1 bowl of red roses on two back flat commodes). On O.P. commode—silver coffee tray (on it—syphon of soda, 3 tumblers, decanter of whisky). 1 small marble-top table (on it—bronze figure of boy, matches and ash-tray); small end of chaise lounge, large arm of chaise lounge, medium gilt Louis couch (on it—1 "Standard" newspaper); 5 single gilt chairs; 1 large buhl writing-desk (on it—brown leather set of writing materials, silver ink-stand, 2 pens, 1 pencil, 1 small glass vase of red roses, silver cigarette-box and cigarettes, matches and ashtray, foreign telegraph forms); 1 centre-piece of chaise lounge; 2 pairs of yellow curtains and pelmets. In P.S. backing—1 tapestry Louis armchair. 3 small pictures on backing.

Stand-bys, P.S.:
Small silver salver with unopened letters, grand piano, 3 musicstands and 4 chairs. Written letter for Willie. Cigarettes for Grenham and Willie.

ACT TWO

1 large Turkey carpet; 1 carpet square in back room; green fireplace and kerb, and brasses; large Hepplewhite green couch; 1 occasional table above fireplace (on it — writing-pad, bowl of roses, tall glass vase of delphiniums). On mantelpiece — 1 jewel-case of pearls, matches and ashtray. On table in back room — various newspapers, "The Times" special, and china bowl of delphiniums. 2 large green armchairs. In windows — 1 china vase of yellow roses, 2 paper vases of yellow roses, 1 papier-mâché vase. In O.P. window — 1 large yellow vase of delphiniums; 5 pairs of chintz curtains and valances. 1 tall grandfather clock; 8 red plush single chairs; 4 occasional tables; 1 writing-table (on it — writing materials, china set, 1 glass vase of roses, stamped letters). On centre back table — tantalus, syphon of soda, 3 tumblers, matches and ashtray. On table head of couch — matches, ashtray, cigarette-box and cigarettes, shallow bowl of roses. Outside in garden — 1 long flower-bed with various flowers. On small table O.P., flat — 1 bronze figure of gladiator.

Stand-bys, O.P. side:
Silver teatray, teapot, sugar-basin, cream-jug, 6 cups and saucers, cake-stand with fancy cakes, jam sandwich, bread and butter, knitting, 1 bunch of roses with ribbon, "The Times" newspaper, "Pall Mall," "Evening Standard," silver salver, gent's visiting-card (Mr. John Willocks). Book of stamps for Grenham. Letter for Margot.

ACT THREE

Bouquet of roses, copy of "The Times."

INCIDENTAL MUSIC IN ACT ONE

1. "In Romany"
2. "Wun Lung Tu"
3. "Caravan"
4. "Dancing Honeymoon" } Fox-trots.
5. "Ula-lula-lu"
6. "Lazy Girl" (Valse)

THREE YEARS FROM "THIRTY"
Mike O'Malley

Dramatic Comedy / 4m, 3f / Unit set

This funny, poignant story of a group of 27-year-olds who have known each other since college sold out during its limited run at New York City's Sanford Meisner Theater. Jessica Titus, a frustrated actress living in Boston, has become distraught over local job opportunities and she is feeling trapped in her long standing relationship with her boyfriend Tom. She suddenly decides to pursue her dreams in New York City. Unbeknownst to her, Tom plans to propose on the evening she has chosen to leave him. The ensuing conflict ripples through their lives and the lives of their roommates and friends, leaving all of them to reconsider their careers, the paths of their souls and the questions, demands and definition of commitment.